Susan stiffened as Jerry looked at her. But I've never kissed a boy before, she thought as Jerry's lips gently brushed hers. Her body tingled from the top of her head to the tips of her toes. Her cheeks felt hot and her palms felt damp and clammy.

So that's how it feels, she thought. Do you have the same feeling every time you kiss? Or would it be different with another guy? She couldn't help wondering.

How would she feel if she were kissing Neil?

Dear Readers,

We at Silhouette would like to thank all our readers for your many enthusiastic letters. In direct response to your encouragement, we are now publishing *four* FIRST LOVEs every month.

As always FIRST LOVEs are written especially for and about you—your hopes, your dreams, your ambitions.

Please continue to share your suggestions and comments with us; they play an important part in our pleasing you.

I invite you to write to us at the address below:

Nancy Jackson
Senior Editor
Silhouette Books
P.O. Box 769
New York, N.Y. 10019

LOVE AND HONORS
Oneta Ryan

First Love from Silhouette

Published by Silhouette Books New York

America's Publisher of Contemporary Romance

Other First Loves by Oneta Ryan

Sometime My Love
Tomorrow's Wish
A Time for Us
A New Beginning

 SILHOUETTE BOOKS, a Division of Simon & Schuster, Inc.
1230 Avenue of the Americas, New York, N.Y. 10020

Copyright © 1983 by Oneta Ryan

Distributed by Pocket Books

All rights reserved, including the right to reproduce
this book or portions thereof in any form whatsoever.
For information address Silhouette Books, 1230
Avenue of the Americas, New York, N.Y. 10020

ISBN: 0-671-53372-X

First Silhouette Books printing November, 1983

10 9 8 7 6 5 4 3 2 1

America's Publisher of Contemporary Romance

Printed in the U.S.A.

For
Rosemary and Ruth Ann

1

How about here?" Susan Harris asked, dropping her beach umbrella and canvas bag at her side. "I think this is the best spot we're going to get today."

"I think you're right," Pam Edwards said. "I guess everybody had the same idea we had." She grinned at Susan. "No wonder it sounded so right when I thought it."

"You're so modest," Susan said. "Shy and retiring. That's what I've always liked about you, Pam." Susan struggled with the giant umbrella, forcing her long blond tresses out of her eyes. She glanced at Pam's feet and then at her friend's face. "Well, 'Shy and

Retiring.' Are you going to help me with this monster, or are you going to stand there gawking until I get it set up?"

"Do I have a choice?"

"No."

"I didn't think so."

Susan guided the operation, and when the umbrella was open, she and Pam forced it into the golden sand. She took an old quilt from her canvas bag and spread it along the circle of shade that the umbrella provided.

"That's good enough," Pam said, sitting on the quilt and folding her legs. She threw open a corner of the quilt beside her. "It doesn't have to be perfect. Not for me, anyway."

"It doesn't have to be perfect for me, either," Susan said. "But if we've got a quilt to sit on, I want to sit on it. Not on the sand."

Susan glanced at the long stretch of golden sand ahead of them and watched as the ocean licked at the people playing at the water's edge. "I bet everybody we know is on this island today," she said, sitting on the quilt beside Pam.

"Are you kidding? Be real. You know everybody within fifteen miles of St. Augustine is on this beach today. It's the last day of freedom for nine months." Pam pulled a bottle of suntan oil from her bag. "Yes. Tomorrow it's hello sallow, good-bye tan."

A heady aroma of coconut mixed with vanilla glided from the open bottle in Pam's hand and mingled with the salty ocean breeze. "At least you get a tan every summer," Susan said. "There are those of us who don't." Susan applied a white, medicinal-smelling liquid to her legs, arms and face. "Blond hair and blue eyes equal burn and peel. I learned that a long time ago." She stuffed her long blond hair up under a bandana scarf and applied the prescription sunscreen to her neck and shoulders.

"It doesn't seem fair to live within ten miles of St. Augustine and not be able to tan," Pam said. "It really doesn't seem fair. I feel for you."

Susan smiled. That wasn't all that didn't seem fair to her lately. She smoothed the sunscreen over her body and tried not to think the thoughts that had haunted her all summer; but try as she might, they came and captured her mind again. What would tomorrow be like? Sure. She and Pam would be in a different school. High school, not junior high any longer. But that wasn't going to be the only thing that would be different. She knew that, even though Pam didn't. That letter the school sent home with her last spring was going to make things different. If only her mother hadn't signed and approved it. But she had signed it. Had been happy to approve it.

"Earth calling Susan, earth calling Susan. Come in, Susan."

Susan glanced at Pam.

"What were you thinking? I thought you were going to rub your skin off."

"Oh, I guess I was just thinking about tomorrow." Susan wondered again, as she had off and on all summer, just what that letter meant. What would it be like to be in classes for the "gifted."

"Yeah. I know what you mean. I've been thinking about the first day of high school for a long time."

"We've talked about it all summer," Susan said. "Now that it's finally here, what have you decided?"

Pam fluffed her short, brown, curly hair with her fingertips. "I'm not sure I've made a decision on anything, really. I know it's going to be fun, though. High school is a lot more fun than junior high."

"You been there before?"

"No. But Karen has. A couple of weeks ago before she went back to college, she told me to have a great time in high school. That it was a really fun time for her." Pam grinned and wrapped her arms around her knees. "It was about then that Mom came into the room and said for me not to have as good a time as Karen did in high school. Mom said she'd like for my grades to be better than Karen's."

"I thought Karen did okay. She got into college."

"She got into college, but she's no brain, like some people we know," Pam said, staring into Susan's eyes.

"And what's that supposed to mean?"

"You know. Be real. I am a carbon copy of my sister. I'll probably go through high school making *B*'s and *C*'s like she did. You, a person who never has to worry about grades, will hit the steps of any college you want, greeted by open arms."

"Now, *you* be real."

"I am," Pam said enthusiastically. She got on her knees and placed her hands in front of her. "Picture this. Graduation. Then summer. Then college. There I'll be on the college steps, down on my hands and knees, saying, 'Please, oh, please let me in.' And you, brainy Susan, will walk up and the college administrators will fling open the doors, take you by the arms and whisk you inside, saying, 'Susan. We've been waiting for you. Come right in. You may study whatever you want.' I can see it all now."

"I think your visions are a little warped, Pam." Susan stretched out on her stomach, facing the ocean. "You make me sound like some sort of freak. Thanks a lot. Best friends are for making you feel good."

Pam stretched out on the quilt beside Susan. "I didn't mean anything by what I said. Gosh, Susan. You know what everybody says about me. I'm always saying things before I think."

"I think you like that reputation."

Pam giggled. "Well, it does get me out of some messes once in a while."

"It gets you into some, too."

"Well, what I really meant is that you should be glad you're brainy. I mean, you already know what you want to be. You've known since we were kids that you wanted to go to college and be a veterinarian." Pam propped her elbows on the quilt and cradled her chin in her palms. "Do you realize that in all those years I've gone through about a million occupations? First I was going to be a teacher, then a nurse, then I jumped from nurse to superstar. I think that was always my favorite. I dumped that one when I realized that I have no talent. In anything. It's sad. Really sad." Pam pulled on the front of her bikini top and shifted her position on the quilt. "I mean, if you really think about it, you and I are as different as day and night.

I'm surprised we've stayed best friends all of these years."

Different. The one thing Susan didn't want to be. "We aren't that different," she said. She thought about the letter once again, and about the words "classes for the gifted." "I think the reason we've stayed best friends for so long is because we've been in most of the same classes since fourth grade. Don't you?"

"I guess."

Susan wondered if they would remain best friends once school started. She wondered if "gifted" meant being in a completely different set of classes from other kids, or if it meant being in some classes that were different and some classes that were the same.

"Pam. Do you think we'd still be best friends if we weren't in any classes together?"

Pam looked at Susan and frowned. "Of course. Don't you?"

"Sure," Susan said hesitantly. "At least, I'd hope you'd still be my best friend. You know that in high school there'll be a lot of different classes to choose from, and we may not get in any of each other's classes."

"Oh, now I get it," Pam said, as though a new thought had popped into her head. "You're getting crazy because you think you might get stuck in one of those experimental classes like you did when we were in the seventh grade."

Susan's heart pounded wildly. How did she know I was thinking about that class? Does she know about these special classes? I didn't tell her. How would she know?

"Well, if that's what you're worrying about, forget it," Pam said, not waiting for Susan to speak. "I felt sorry for you in that math class. You all were like guinea pigs. We made it through that year, and we weren't in many classes together."

"I guess you're right," Susan said. The thought of being in experimental classes again bothered her. Gifted classes couldn't be as bad as that.

"Hey. Remember when we were in elementary school?" Pam asked. "Remember, when we got into our reading groups the teacher would divide us into three groups. One teacher we had divided us into the A group, the B group and the C group. Everybody knew that the A group you were in were the brains."

"Well, why wouldn't they know? That was easy." Susan smiled. "Then there was Miss Hill, who divided us into the lemon, orange and lime groups."

"She was clever. Everybody thought the lemon group was going to be the worst," Pam said. "But we all knew different when you and the other regulars were lemons."

"You have to admit, she gave it a good try."

"The one I liked the best was Mrs. Saunders. She used colors and mixed the kids a little better. Remember? There were the green, blue and purple groups. Green was the group to be in. I was a blue."

"I was a green."

"I know. That's how I figured out the order of things." Pam took a deep breath and let it out slowly. "I just love the smell of the ocean. Fish, moss, salt, birds, wet sand. Sounds gross, doesn't it? I love it, though. I can't help it."

"I know what you mean," Susan said. "I've been coming to Anastasia Island since I was a little kid." Susan rolled over on her back and shaded her eyes with her arm. The heat from the sun and the sand wrapped her like a blanket, and her thoughts drifted back over the years to a time when she was very young. A time when her parents used to bring her to the friendly island beach. A time before the boating accident that claimed her father's life.

"You'd think I'd never want to come here again," Susan whispered, unaware that she'd verbalized the thought.

"What? Did you say something to me?"

Susan sat up and stared out across the water. "I was just talking to myself. I was remembering when Mom and Dad and I used to come to this beach."

"I bet you miss your dad. I can't imagine."

"I can't say that I miss him. I don't really remember having him around. I was only two when he died." Susan shrugged her shoulders. "After living with only my mom for thirteen years, it seems that she and I are the way a family is supposed to be. Sometimes I wonder what things are like for you, having a dad around the house all of the time."

Pam tilted her head. "I never thought of it that way. But I can see what you mean." She scratched at a spot beneath her thick brown hair. "This conversation is getting too heavy for me. I'm going to get some water. I need to cool off. You coming?"

"No. You go ahead. We're going to be here all afternoon, and if I start playing games with that sun now, it's going to be pain city tomorrow." Susan scooted under the umbrella's shade, inching closer to the protective canvas. "I'm going to stay here where it's safe for a while longer. I'll try the water after we've had time to really get hot."

"I'm hot enough now." Pam stood and adjusted her bikini, then ran across the hot sand toward the water. She jumped and stepped through white-capped waves at the shoreline and swam out toward the blue-green depths of the ocean. "It's great, Susan," she yelled. "Come on in."

Susan slowly and deliberately shook her head. Then she pulled her paperback copy of *Gone With the Wind* from her beach bag and held it in the air.

Pam motioned a sign of disapproval and disappointment, then turned her back on Susan.

"It's a great book," Susan said to herself more than to Pam. She stretched out on her back once again and smoothed her blue one-piece bathing suit across her side and stomach. When you burn, you can't make it through an afternoon on the beach without a book, Susan thought. A book, a quilt, an umbrella, a cooler of cola and food. She laughed inwardly at herself and Pam. You'd think we had planned to spend a week.

Susan didn't know if it was the strange coolness of the breeze or the slamming of the ice chest lid that had awakened her, but when she opened her eyes, she saw Pam sitting on a corner of the quilt, dripping wet, with a cola in one hand and a sandwich in the other.

"It's about time you woke up," Pam said, still chewing on the bit of sandwich in her mouth. "You're a lot of fun to go to the beach with."

"How long have I been asleep?"

"I don't know. Probably an hour. I've been in the water most of the time."

Susan returned *Gone With the Wind* to her bag so it wouldn't get wet. "I guess it was the warm sand and the heat from the sun on this canvas umbrella that made me fall asleep. I don't remember getting through a full page of my book."

"You are the only person I know who brings a book to the beach. You know that, don't you?" Pam gulped the cola. "I have never taken a book to the beach. Books are for libraries."

"Libraries are for checking out books and taking them with you to the beach."

"Whatever. All I know, Susan, is that while you were sleeping, you missed the cutest hunk I've ever seen. I mean it. Tall, brown hair—almost black—brown eyes, the most beautiful tan you've ever seen."

"And twenty years old, no doubt."

"No. That was the best part. I think he was about our age."

"If he was our age, and we've never seen him, that means that he's a tourist. You know that. St. Augustine is full of tourists this time of the year. And I bet half of them cross the Bridge of Lions and come over here to this beach. People who don't live around the Atlantic Ocean always go see it when they are close to it on vacation. He was a tourist."

"So what? He was a cutie. A real cutie."

Susan lifted the lid on the ice chest and pulled a cola from the chipped ice. "I don't know why you're getting crazy over a guy you don't know anyway. I thought you and Roger were on the verge of going together."

"Going with and being on the verge of are two different things." Pam raised her eyebrows into the tight wet curls on her forehead. "I am crazy about Roger, though. That cutie I saw was just that. A cutie. He and I weren't on the same team. We weren't even in the same ball park."

"You're babbling again."

"I know. But there are some things you know. Like I know that Roger and I are just right for each other. Cutie and I would never have made it. No vibes. Well, we just wouldn't have made it, that's all. I decided to get hold of myself and not fling myself at his feet to try to capture his attention, needless to say his affections."

Susan laughed, unable to hold it inside any longer. "A wise move." She giggled. "I'm glad you came to your senses. You always do."

"Yeah. Five minutes before it's too late." Pam gulped the last bite of sandwich. "I wish we'd see Roger and Jerry here today. That'd be great."

"Jerry told me that he and his parents were going to Jacksonville today to visit his grandmother."

"Did he call you and tell you that?" Pam asked. "Did he really call you?"

"Pam. Get hold of yourself. I saw him outside when I was loading the umbrella into the car. I guess he had been helping his dad load their car. He just saw me and walked over and started talking. After all, four houses down is not that big of a deal."

"I wish I only lived four houses away from Roger. I bet we'd be going together now for sure."

"Or you'd be on his doorstep saying 'Please, oh, please.'"

"I probably would."

A long wide shadow moved across the sand

and out over the water, cooling the breeze as it moved.

"I bet it's going to rain again," Pam said. "Why does it have to rain like this every afternoon I am on the beach?"

"It's been raining like this every afternoon this week."

"Well, move over," Pam said, moving closer to the umbrella's core. "I'm just not going to let a little rain spoil my last day of freedom."

The words had no sooner left Pam's lips when large drops of rain slowly but steadily pelted the canvas umbrella.

"My mom will be here to pick us up if it doesn't stop soon," Susan said. "She's funny about stuff like that."

"It'll stop. It has to."

Susan watched the drops hit the water and make tiny wet craters in the sand. The last day of freedom. Pam's words rang in Susan's ears. For me, it might really be the last day of freedom. Classes for the gifted, Susan thought. Why don't they just divide us into groups as they've always done? A smile stole across her lips as she pictured a high school English class being divided into reading groups. I'd probably be a green again, Susan thought whimsically. And Pam would still be a blue.

Susan thought about her goal to become a veterinarian. Whatever gifted classes are, they might help her get into college, might make it easier for her to get into vet school.

As quickly as the rain had started, it stopped. A dark gray cloud continued to hang over Anastasia Island, but the rain no longer chased the visitors along the beach.

"What if we don't get into each other's classes this year?" Susan asked.

Pam turned her gaze from the cloudy sky to Susan. "What if we don't? We will."

"But what if we don't? There'll be a lot more kids at Castleview High than there were at Barkley J. H. I think there's a very real possibility that we won't have many classes together. Maybe none," Susan said.

"Susan. We learned that 'what if' game in seventh grade, and you still spring it on me. Aren't you ever going to get over it?"

"Sometimes it helps you think. Why do you think they bothered to try to teach it to us?" Susan crossed her legs in front of her and stared at Pam. "Now, come on. Play it. What if we aren't in any classes together this year?"

"If we aren't, we aren't. Guess there isn't much we can do about it."

"Do you think we'd still be best friends?"

"Susan. You're being crazy. Of course we'd still be best friends. Being best friends has nothing to do with school." Pam dug her toes into the sand, inching deeper and deeper until the tops of her feet were buried. "Gosh, sometimes you really get me. For a brain, sometimes yours doesn't work very well."

"What do you mean?"

"Duh, Susan. Be real." Pam shook the sand from her feet and stared Susan in the eye. "I'm sure I wouldn't be best friends with you if we weren't in each other's classes. Really! We've only got everything in the world going for us. We've been best friends since we were little. And now that we're grown, we've got boyfriends. I think of Roger as a boyfriend, anyway. Don't you think of Jerry as a boyfriend?"

Susan thought for an instant and nodded, still unsure as to whether she thought of Jerry as a boyfriend or not. She liked him. She'd really grown to like him more over this past summer than ever before. But boyfriend? She wondered if he thought of her as a girlfriend.

"Boyfriends mean dating," Pam continued. "And almost as good as dating is driver's ed. We get to sign up for driver's ed and that means that before long, all of us will be learning to drive." Pam moved her arms and hands as rapidly as she talked, trying to emphasize her message. "That's it, Susan. We are all—you, me, Roger and Jerry—all going to have to sign up for driver's ed at the same time and we'll all get the same training car. Then we can all go down and take the written test at the same time, and we'll all get our driver's permit on the same day." She clapped her hands together in front of her. "This is such a terrific idea, I'm surprised I thought of it. Why didn't you think of it? You're the A student here."

Susan laughed at Pam's animated gestures. "I might have thought of it if you hadn't been going crazy. I had to keep watching you to see what you were going to do next. I thought you might take off and fly away with those pelicans out there on that sand bar at any moment."

"I feel like flying," Pam said. "This might be my last day of freedom, but I'm going to make tomorrow my first day of fun. High school is going to be great for us. I just know it is. Don't you?"

"Sure," Susan said. "Tomorrow we can go to school together and pick up our schedules. Then, I guess we'll just take it from there."

"And when they announce the time for

driver's ed sign-up, we'll all go together and do it."

"Right."

The dark cloud that had hovered over the island moved away from the sun's path, and once again the beach was filled with an almost blinding glow.

2

Susan shut off the alarm on her clock radio and saw the glowing rays of sunlight playing hide-and-seek with her bedroom curtains.

This is it, she thought, throwing back the crisp cotton sheet. The first day of high school, and the day I'm finally going to find out what being in "gifted" classes really means. "I bet knowing isn't half as bad as not knowing," she said to herself as she walked into the bathroom.

Susan showered and blew her hair dry, then set it on hot curlers. As she rolled the last curler to her head, she heard the radio disc jockey announce that the high tempera-

ture for the Matanzas Bay area was expected
to be ninety-one degrees.

"Ninety-one," Susan said. One thing
about living near the Florida coast, she
thought. It's almost always warm, and almost
always humid.

Susan walked to her closet to find something to wear. It had to be just right. Not too
plain, but not too fancy, either. She opened
the closet door and stared at the rack of
shirts, blouses and dresses. Jeans are a must,
she decided, pulling a new pair of jeans from
the dresser drawer inside her closet. It
doesn't matter if it's one hundred and one
today, Susan thought, easing the jeans over
her slender hips; a girl just can't wear a dress
on the first day of school.

Without giving the matter another
thought, she took a short-sleeve knit shirt
from the dresser drawer and slipped it over
her head in one fluid motion.

Seating herself in front of the mirror,
Susan carefully applied just the right shades
of eyeshadow and makeup to complement
her outfit and highlight her sapphire-blue
eyes. When she pulled the hot rollers from
her hair, her long golden locks bounced
freely across her shoulders to the middle of
her back. Gently, she brushed her hair, being
careful not to brush out the freshly set curls.

Susan glanced at her total appearance, turning and twisting in front of the mirror. The new jeans made her feel fresh and new, and the knit shirt was one of her favorites. It gave her a feeling of confidence and security in knowing that the best she could do with her appearance was really pretty good after all.

"You look kinda cute," she said to her reflection. "Not bad." She clenched her teeth and looked at them closely, wondering if she needed to brush them one more time, just to be on the safe side. How embarrassing it would be to have something caught in your teeth and not know it, especially on the first day of school!

Susan glanced around the room, not knowing for sure what she was looking for or hoping to find. "I guess this is it," she whispered. Her heart picked up tempo as she gathered her notebook and ball-point pens from the corner of her desk. "Calm yourself, girl. It's just the first day of high school. You aren't going on national television."

She surveyed the room one final time, scanning the posters of her favorite entertainers that were mounted on two walls. The posters were so close together that Susan could hardly see any patches of the periwinkle-blue wall around them. The other two walls were fairly uncluttered except for the college and university pennants and a grouping of watercolors that her mother had painted.

Susan's gaze traveled to the large window and the blue and white gingham curtains that she'd pulled back to let in the morning sun. The only visible mess in the room at all was the top of the dresser, with makeup Susan had just used still scattered across the top.

"I'll clean that off later," she said, glancing at the clock radio beside the bed. "It's time to go."

Susan walked out of her bedroom and closed the door behind her. Heading for the aroma of freshly brewed coffee that seemed to float out of the kitchen, she smiled as she thought about her mother. Her mother didn't fit the "mother" mold. All other mothers were—well, they were mothers who did motherly things like going to the grocery and cleaning the house. But Susan felt that her mom was different, and she admitted to herself more often now as she grew older that she liked the difference. Sure, Patty Harris went to the grocery and cleaned house, but she was also a public relations woman, and she painted watercolor landscapes for a hobby. She's a terrific mom, Susan thought, bounding into the kitchen. And a terrific dad.

"Morning, Mom."

"Good morning." Patty Harris folded her newspaper and placed it beside her coffee cup. She paused for a moment and then looked at Susan with a hint of suspicion in her eye. "What are you grinning about? Is my head on crooked or something?" she asked, toying with a strand of honey-blond hair at her temple.

Susan placed her notebook on the corner of the kitchen table. "No. Your head's on pretty straight. That's one thing I've always liked about you, Mom. You're a pretty to-gether old gal."

"Easy on the old, young lady. But thanks for the compliment anyway."

"You know," Susan said, thoughtfully. "You aren't like anyone else's mother I know."

"Oh, yeah? What makes you say that?"

"Well, look at you. Here you sit in your tailored business suit, reading the morning newspaper, drinking coffee and getting ready for a hard day at the office. Then when you come home, you'll put on those horrid old jeans with the hole that you never seem to find time to patch, you'll put on that paint-splattered used-to-be-white sweatshirt and you'll paint awhile on that seascape you've been working on. Real mothers don't do those things. They yell at their kids."

"Maybe I've been doing something wrong. Tell me more. And just what do real mothers yell at their kids about?"

"Oh, you know. The usual stuff. Not cleaning their room, not doing their homework. You know."

"Well, if I yelled every time your room wasn't clean enough to suit me, I wouldn't have a voice left at all. It's your room. If you don't mind the clutter, I don't know why I should. It's like my painting room. Just close the door and you can pretend that the clutter doesn't exist." She poured herself another cup of coffee. "I probably would yell if you didn't do your homework. But you always do."

Susan looked at her without saying a word.

"I guess you aren't like anyone else's child I know, either. You're a pretty neat kid," Patty Harris said, sipping her coffee. "I think we make a good pair."

"Right, Mom," Susan said lightly. She walked to the cabinet and reached for a slice of bread for toast before she remembered that her teeth were television-commercial clean. She placed the slice of bread back in the wrapper and glanced admiringly at her mother. Her mother's hair was a little darker than Susan's, but she had the same sapphire-blue eyes and the same slender build. Susan wondered if she would look like her mother when she reached the age of thirty-five. Twenty years. Somehow it seemed too far away to even imagine.

Pouring herself a glass of milk, Susan sat at the table across from her mother. "About ready?"

"I'm waiting on you. Aren't you going to eat something?"

Susan glanced at the kitchen clock. "We don't have time. I told Pam that we'd pick her up at seven-fifteen."

"We better get going then." Patty placed her coffee cup in the sink and filled it with water. "I can't wait for you to find out what the gifted classes are all about," she said. "I bet you and Pam talked about it all day yesterday, didn't you?"

Susan's heart stopped at the mention of Pam and gifted classes all in the same sentence. A lump caught in her throat. How do you tell your mother that you didn't tell your best friend about something like this? she wondered.

"Mom," Susan began hesitantly, "I didn't tell Pam about the classes." The carefree feeling that had embraced the bright yellow kitchen moments earlier no longer hung in the air. "See, those gifted classes are going to make me different from everybody else. And . . ." Susan sighed. "Well, I just don't want to be different. I want to go to classes—normal classes—like everybody else. I didn't tell anybody about this. Who knows? Maybe no one will ever find out." She gave her mother a pleading glance. "Please don't mention this to my friends. I'll handle things. Okay?"

Patty Harris was silent for a moment. "But it's something you should be proud of, Susan."

"I knew you were going to say that. Mothers always say stuff like that."

"But you just told me that I wasn't like all the other mothers you knew."

"You aren't. But you aren't like my friends, either. We are a group."

"I'm not in your group," her mother said, placing her hand on Susan's shoulder. "But I always thought I was your friend."

Susan smiled at her. "You are, Mom. But I want to handle this my way. Okay?"

"I don't understand. But, okay."

Susan breathed a sigh of relief. She finished her milk and placed the glass in the sink. "C'mon. We've got to hit it."

The two-mile ride to Castleview High

didn't take long, and when her mother pulled the car to a stop in front of the school, Susan took a deep breath and told herself one more time that this was going to be one of those "brighter" days.

"Have a good day," Patty Harris said as Susan and Pam slid out of the front seat of the car.

Susan glanced over her shoulder at her mother and winked. "I will, Mom. I will." She closed the car door and hurried to catch up with Pam, who had already started for the front door.

There were tables set up all through the lobby with grade and alphabet designations above each. Susan found the table marked "10—G thru L" and picked up her schedule without having to wait.

She stepped out of the flow of student traffic to a secluded place by some lockers before opening her schedule packet. If I have to be in gifted classes, please don't have it printed on everything in here, Susan thought, breaking the seal on the manila envelope.

"Susan. What have you got?" Pam rushed toward Susan, her white schedule card visible in her hand.

"I'm looking. I'm looking." Susan held her

breath and pulled the white card from the manila envelope. Quickly, she glanced at the face of the card. She breathed a small sigh of relief when she saw that her schedule card appeared to be no different than Pam's. The only difference was that none of the classes on either card appeared in the same time slots.

"Our worst fear has come true," Pam shrieked. "I can't believe this." She glanced at Susan and frowned. "You didn't know this? I mean, we talked about this yesterday, but you didn't know for sure that we weren't going to be in each other's classes, did you?"

"No," Susan said. "I knew there was a possibility that we wouldn't be in some classes. Like my Spanish and your art. But you would have thought we could have at least had phys ed together."

"Phys ed. Look at that. You lucked out and got sixth hour p.e. Do you realize that there are people in this building, in this hallway, who would kill for sixth hour p.e.? And, I might be one of them."

Susan grinned. "Get a grip on yourself. It's not worth killing for, I'm pretty sure."

"I think I'll . . ." Pam's voice trailed off and she turned away from Susan as she stared down the hallway at a crowd of students. She quickly turned to Susan and grabbed her arm. "Do you know who that was?"

"Who who was?"

"Him. That guy. See down there at the end of the hall. Tall, the one wearing that white knit shirt?"

"I see the back of some guy who's wearing a white shirt."

"That's him. That's cutie."

Susan placed her palm on Pam's forehead. "Are you feeling all right?"

"Cutie? You know. That guy I saw on the beach yesterday while you were asleep. I'm telling you, Susan, if you had seen him, you'd be more excited that he's a real live person like we are and not a tourist."

"Do the words Roger Dalton mean anything to you?"

"Going with and being on the verge of are two different things, remember?"

"True. But I don't know what you're getting so excited about. You said that guy wasn't in your league. If he isn't in our league, that makes him equivalent to a tourist again—not a real live person like we are."

"Such a way with words," Pam said, twirling a short brown curl behind her ear. "You have such a precise way of getting my thoughts together. How do you do that?"

"Years of experience, my dear. Years of experience." Susan smiled and tried to pretend that she wasn't nervous about the day ahead. "I think we better set our years of experience together aside and get on with trying to find these classes. Don't you?"

Pam glanced at the large round clock that was mounted on the wall across from them. "I guess we better. In twenty minutes, classes will begin. I'd like to find Roger if I could before I have to go to class." Pam glanced at her schedule card. "I've got to go to two-thirteen. Biology. Yeck. Can't you just imagine what it's going to be like cutting on frogs and worms at eight o'clock in the morning? I think I'm going to be sick."

"I've got it fourth hour. Right after lunch. I don't know which would be worse," Susan said.

"Me either." Pam pushed her schedule card into her purse. "Look for me at lunch and I'll look for you. Maybe we can have a few minutes together then."

"I hope so," Susan agreed enthusiastically.

"If I miss you then, look for me at the front door after school."

Susan nodded as Pam walked down the hall away from her. I'll look for you, she thought. You can be sure I'll look for you.

She glanced at her schedule and then looked up and down the hall. History. Room 105. "Here goes," she sighed, turning to her left and walking in the direction opposite from Pam.

Wandering through the hall, Susan noticed many faces that were familiar to her and many more that were unfamiliar. She glanced only occasionally at the numbers above the classroom doors, hoping that she didn't appear to be a little lost sophomore trying to find a class on the first day of school.

When Susan walked into room 105, she was surprised to see several students whom she recognized from junior high and elementary school. She knew them, but none of them were really in the group that she and Pam considered themselves to be in.

Susan walked toward the back of the room and took a seat on the back row. As her gaze traveled over the students she recognized, a smile filled her face. I should have known, she thought. They're greens. Every one of them was in that sixth-grade reading group. I guess we have been divided into groups. Just on a broader scale.

Susan glanced at each student who walked into the room. Some were new faces, but of the students whom she knew, each was a green. I wonder how they feel about these gifted classes, Susan thought. That's one thing I hadn't thought about before. There's more than one of us in here.

Most of the desks in the front of the room filled rapidly. With just a few minutes remaining before classes were to start, Susan noticed a tall, thin girl walking toward her. She recognized the girl. She was a green, too. But she'd changed over the summer. So much that Susan hardly recognized Gina Tate.

Gina's short red hair was now shoulder length but still looked as though it was supposed to be combed in a particular style and had chosen to do as it pleased instead. Her green eyes were framed with gold-rimmed glasses, and as she drew closer, Susan could see that the summer sun had intensified the reddish brown freckles that splashed across Gina's nose and cheeks like raindrops falling on dry summer sidewalks.

Gina slipped into the empty desk beside Susan and smiled. "Hi."

"Hi," Susan said, amazed that Gina spoke to her.

Gina made a place for her notebook and took a pen from her purse and placed it in the slot in the desk for pens and pencils. She reminded Susan of when they were greens and tried to please their teacher by sitting tall and straight in their chairs with their feet crossed at the ankles and their hands folded on top of their desks. Somehow, Susan expected to see Gina fold her hands at any moment.

Glancing around the room, Gina shifted in her desk. Her gaze stopped at Susan. "It's kind of scary being in a new school, isn't it? I don't have any idea where anything is. Do you?"

"Not at all," Susan said without thinking. She smiled at Gina. She's nervous, too, Susan thought. Just like me, I'll bet. Nervous and wondering what's going to happen next.

Susan basked in the knowledge that she was no longer alone. The girl beside her felt the same way she did. Probably feels strange being in gifted classes, too, she told herself.

"Are you carrying some hard classes?" Gina asked. She held her schedule in her hand and looked as though she wanted to compare notes with Susan.

Susan shrugged her shoulders and tried to act casual. "I guess I'll know by the end of the day how hard they are." She pulled her card from her purse and showed it to Gina.

At first glance, Susan couldn't believe her

eyes. Everything was the same except for fifth hour.

"Looks like the only thing we didn't agree on was whether to take Spanish or French," Gina said, pointing out that their foreign language classes were the only discrepancies on the cards.

"Yeah," Susan said, her heart soaring at the realization that Gina Tate would be in almost all of her classes. She heard the bell ring and saw the teacher enter the classroom. I'm not going to have to be alone all day today after all, she thought.

As the teacher took his place at the front of the class, Susan's gaze traveled from Gina around the room. Suddenly her gaze settled on the boy sitting to her right. A white knit shirt hugged his broad shoulders, and for a moment Susan tried to visualize the boy Pam had pointed out to her in the hallway earlier.

Out of the corner of her eye, Susan stared at the boy's deep brown eyes and thick black lashes. His hair was such a dark brown that it was almost black, and his tanned skin drew attention to his eyes and hair as a fine frame does to an even finer painting.

Susan heard the teacher begin to talk from someplace far away, but try as she might, she couldn't take her attention away from the boy. Who are you? she wondered.

Almost as if the boy had read her mind, he turned and looked at Susan, then smiled.

Instantly, her face burned with embarrassment and she looked away.

Susan focused her thoughts on the teacher and read the man's name on the blackboard. Mr. Fleming. She propped her chin in her hand and tried to keep her thoughts from wandering. Her body began to tingle and her heart raced in a way that she'd never experienced before. Could this be happening because of him? she wondered, glancing at the boy beside her. Probably. Pam had been right. He was definitely the cutest boy she'd ever seen.

Mr. Fleming continued to talk from his position in the front of the room, and it wasn't until he mentioned the word *gifted* that Susan was able to give her full attention to the man.

"You students have been tagged as 'gifted,'" Mr. Fleming said. "And as gifted students, you will find that these special classes you've been assigned to will be different from some of the classes your friends might be enrolled in; and in some ways, the classes will be the same." He slipped his hand into his coat pocket and removed a piece of chalk and rolled it between his fingers as he talked.

"This program is new to Castleview High this year. We're all very excited about the program," he said. "And we're excited about having you in it."

Susan watched the man toy with the chalk and wondered if he was as nervous as she was.

"You've been selected for this program based on aptitude test scores over the past three years," Mr. Fleming continued. "Each of you has consistently scored in the ninety-seven, ninety-eight or ninety-nine percentile range." He placed the chalk on the blackboard and gripped the podium with both hands as he stood behind it. "That's very good."

That depends on how you look at it, Susan thought. College, she reminded herself. Think about how it will look when you're trying to get an academic scholarship into college.

Mr. Fleming told the class about how his history class would be taught, and how the gifted program included their history, English and geometry classes.

"There won't be any extensive testing for this group this year. Aptitude testing, that is," he said, smiling. "However, there will be a battery of tests given to you the second and third weeks of school. This is simply a double check for us to be sure that each of you really does belong in this program."

More tests, Susan thought glumly. Oh, well, they couldn't be much harder than all the other tests she had taken.

"Beginning the second week of school, and during the third week, you will be scheduled for tests three mornings each week at seven o'clock. A total of six half-hour tests will be given," Mr. Fleming said. "If any of you know of a conflict in your schedule preventing you from taking the tests at that time, please let me know as soon as possible and I'll try to work out special arrangements for you."

Susan thought for a minute and couldn't think of any reason to change the testing times herself. Testing at seven simply would mean that her mother would have to take her to school early on those days. And that would mean that Pam probably wouldn't ride with them. But for six days, it wouldn't be so bad.

Mr. Fleming used the remainder of the class period to tell them everything he thought they would need to know about his class and the gifted program.

Susan had to admit that he was a likable

person, even though he wasn't that handsome. For almost an hour she'd watched him adjust his horn-rimmed glasses that rested on a nose that looked as though it belonged on a much larger man. He spoke with a slight lisp, so faint that when Susan first noticed it at the beginning of the hour, she thought her hearing was off rather than his speech. His pale blue eyes crinkled at the corners when he smiled. Any teacher whose eyes crinkle like that can't be all bad, she thought.

Mr. Fleming turned and glanced at the round clock mounted on the wall behind him. "Just a couple more things before the bell rings," he said. "You are all eligible to join the Honor Society. And I hope that you will consider it. I'm the group's sponsor, and I can tell you that we are going to do some fun things this year. Some of them you could apply as extra credit in this class, and some projects could apply to the history course itself. So give it some thought."

He leafed through the papers on the podium and pulled one to the top. "I was supposed to have read this to you at the beginning of class in our ten-minute homeroom period," he explained, holding the paper in the air. "But I wanted to tell you all of the good stuff about high school and the terrific program you're in first, saving the daily bulletin for last."

Susan listened as he read through a list of several unimportant items, items that she felt were not relevant to her.

"And this final item," he said, "concerns driver's education."

Susan straightened in her seat. All right, she thought. This is going to be great.

"All students wanting to take driver's education must sign up within the next two days in room three-eleven. Driver's education begins Monday—a week from today," Mr. Fleming said, glancing up from the paper, "and it meets at seven o'clock every morning for four weeks."

Seven o'clock? Four weeks? Susan's heart thundered in her chest as Mr. Fleming began to explain.

"Unfortunately, this group will be unable to take driver's ed this semester because of our special testing for the next two weeks. However, those of you who do not want to wait until next semester might want to check into the adult education evening classes. I know that they offer several sections of driver's ed because our day program always has more students wanting to take the program than we can accommodate. I've heard that the evening program is quite good."

Susan felt as though she'd been punched in the stomach. *I knew I probably wouldn't be in any of Pam's classes,* she thought. *But I was really counting on being with everybody in driver's ed.*

She glanced at Gina on her left and then at the boy on her right. Gina seemed to be sitting on the edge of her seat waiting for Mr. Fleming to say more. And the boy on her right. His deep brown eyes reflected a matter-of-fact acceptance of everything Mr. Fleming said.

When the bell rang ending the class, the boy looked Susan's way, grinned and nodded, then hurried out of the room. Susan's heart raced after him.

She followed Gina out of the classroom and thought about Pam, Roger and Jerry and how they probably had heard the same bulletins this morning. *Unless I come up with a miracle, they'll all be in driver's ed and I'll be taking tests,* she thought.

Susan and Gina wove their way in and out of the crowd of students that filled the narrow hallways. Suddenly, she remembered. Mr.

Fleming said that if any of them had a conflict and couldn't take the tests at seven, he would work out something else. Susan grinned to herself. She would talk to her mother about it that evening. She could take driver's ed with Pam at seven and get her tests rescheduled to a different time.

3

When the final bell sounded, Susan couldn't believe that the day was really over. The day had been long, with English, geometry, biology and Spanish following her first-hour history class. Geometry was the worst, Susan thought, but this last hour has been the most miserable.

"If I had to sit in this smelly room much longer, I think I'd die," Susan said as she and Gina rose from their seated positions on the gym's hardwood floor.

"I know," Gina said. "How could a big room like this get so smelly and hot when all we did was just sit here and listen to the teacher give us instructions all hour?"

"This smell is probably left over from last year," Susan said.

Gina nodded and stepped out into the hallway ahead of Susan.

"You have to admit," Susan went on, "gyms have a smell all their own. It's kind of like the smell of a new car. Distinct. Only with gyms it's not so classy."

Gina laughed and shifted her books to one arm. She pushed her glasses up on her nose with her free hand. "You're funny." She stopped laughing for a second and held up her hand in defense. "I don't mean you're funny. I mean you have a weird sense of humor."

Susan smiled at her. "I don't think I like having a weird sense of humor any better than being funny."

"I guess what I'm trying to say is that I'm really glad we have so many classes together. I've never been able to make friends very easily, and I know you probably don't think of me as your friend or anything after one day. I mean, I know you and Pam are friends, but it's been a lot of fun being in your classes and hanging around with you today."

"Don't be silly," Susan said. She looked at Gina curiously, remembering how their morning began. "This morning in home-room, you came in and sat beside me and

said 'hi.' I call that being pretty friendly.
Besides, the only reason we haven't been
friends before is because we've never had
that many classes together and really haven't
gotten to know each other. You're a pretty
outgoing girl."

Gina smiled and turned away bashfully.
Then she looked at Susan and said, "That
was part of my 'On Starting High School
plan.' I told myself yesterday that I was going
to start school today and make myself do
something besides sit in class and do my
sponge impression."

"Sponge?"

"Yeah. Stare at the teacher and soak up
everything he says. It's a real detriment at
times. Do you know what it's like to be shy
and be one of the smartest girls in your
class?" Gina asked.

Susan nodded.

They entered the lobby and got caught in
the flow of students trying to get to their
lockers and out of the building. Susan
glanced at the faces, searching for Pam, but
she was nowhere in sight.

"You said that you spoke to me because of
some kind of plan you decided on," Susan
said, opening her locker and putting the
books she didn't need for homework inside.
"If I hadn't been friendly back, would you

have chosen somebody else to be your friend today?"

Gina shrugged her shoulders. "Who knows. Probably not. Not today, anyway. That was the second part of my plan. Avoid rejection at all costs."

Susan smiled. "Well, save yourself that worry. I'm glad we're friends. I think it's been great being in your classes today. Especially geometry. That one's going to be a bear."

"I'm not sweating that one as much as I am biology," Gina said. "I've never been any good in science."

Susan glanced at Gina. "You know, it was great having somebody to talk to and be with all day."

"I think so, too."

Susan glanced at the clock overhead and searched the hallways once more for Pam. "I don't know where Pam is." She sighed. "But I've got to run or I'll miss my bus." She slammed the locker door and started for the foyer. "See you tomorrow."

"Yeah. See ya," Gina shouted.

When Susan got off the school bus, she was still wondering what had happened to Pam. They had planned to meet on the bus and ride home together. Maybe she caught a ride with somebody else, Susan thought, as she entered her house.

She walked down the hallway into her bedroom and dropped her books onto her bed. She just had to talk her mother into letting her reschedule those tests so she could take driver's education. She sat on the side of the bed. She didn't know how she would convince her mother, but if she had dinner on the table and waiting for her, she might have a better chance.

Mrs. Harris sat heavily on the kitchen chair. She sighed. "I'm so glad you did this, Susan. I had a terrible day at the office and I'm so tired. I think I'll go lie down and read after we're finished eating." She passed Susan a bowl of green beans. "Unless we have something we need to do tonight."

"No," Susan said. "I don't have anything."

Susan told her about the special tests.

"I don't see that that will be a problem. I need to get some things done at work, anyway. I'll just take you to school early and get to the office early," Patty said.

Susan knew that this was the moment she'd been dreading. "Well, there is a problem, sort of," she said hesitantly. "See, driver's ed classes begin next week, too, and if I don't take them then, I'll have to wait until next semester."

Patty Harris shrugged. "I know that you've been looking forward to learning to drive, but I don't think driver's ed is important enough to reschedule a whole set of tests. Besides, you won't be sixteen until next semester. There's plenty of time."

"But Mom, that's not the point."

"Well, what is the point?" her mother asked.

"The point is that Pam and everybody else are going to take driver's ed this time and I won't get to take it with them."

"*Everybody else* is not in gifted classes," her mother reminded her.

"Yeah, and that's the point. I hate being different. I hate being the one who always makes *A*'s, and I hate not being able to do what everybody else does," Susan said, trying to hold back her tears.

Patty Harris didn't speak. She pushed her plate to one side and her vibrant blue eyes turned a smoky gray. She took a deep breath. "But sometimes you can't be like everybody else," she said. "And I guess to some extent that's my fault. I'm sorry, Susan. But sometimes you have to see things the way I see them."

Susan felt a lecture coming, and she wished she could evaporate.

"It's my responsibility as your mother to see that you're prepared to go out on your own when the time comes," her mother started. "That includes seeing that you get the best education you can, and it includes my providing for you as best I can. Susan, you must see that these classes are important for what you want to do with the rest of your life. You want to become a veterinarian. This is the beginning of that education." She sighed, then shook her head. "There's so much more at stake here than learning to drive with your friends."

A tear slid down Susan's face. "I know, Mom," she said. "It's just that life's so hard at times."

Patty nodded. "It is. And, unfortunately, it doesn't get much easier as you go along." She touched Susan's hand. "When your father died, I didn't know how I was going to raise you. I never dreamed of all the decisions I'd have to make on my own."

Susan found herself feeling sorrier for her mother than she did for herself. She gave her a brief hug before she busied herself clearing the dishes from the table and placing them in the sink.

Finally after the table was cleared and only

her mother's coffee cup remained, her mother spoke.

"I've been thinking. The other day I got an Adult Education Classes brochure in the mail. Seems to me that there were some driver's ed classes in that."

Susan remembered Mr. Fleming mentioning the evening classes now that her mother had.

"What would you think about that?" Mrs. Harris asked. "Evening seems to be a good time. As a matter of fact, I took driver's ed in evening classes when I was in high school."

Susan looked at her curiously.

"Don't look so surprised. We did have cars *way* back then," Patty said, smiling. "And they weren't Model T's."

Their laughter filled the kitchen.

"Well, what do you think about that idea?" her mother prodded.

"I think that might be what I'll do. Taking driver's ed now at night would allow me to take the written test and get my permit at the same time that Pam and the other kids do."

"Exactly."

"Yeah. I think I might do that."

"I still don't understand why you couldn't have waited at the front door for two minutes yesterday and told me that you were getting a ride home with Roger," Susan said as soon as she and Pam stepped out of the car.

"And I still don't understand why you have to take those stupid tests." Pam shifted her books in her arms and stacked her purse on top of them. "Our class doesn't have to take them. At least I don't think we do."

Susan sighed and opened the school door for Pam and herself. "All I know is that Mr. Fleming said we had to take some tests and that any of us who wanted to take driver's ed had to take it at night or wait until next semester. I decided to take it at night so I could get my permit when you do."

"Good idea! You always figure out the right thing to do," she said. "Did I tell you already that Roger and Jerry are in almost all of my classes?"

"Yes." Susan felt relief trickle through her. Maybe she could just drop the subject of tests and get on to something else, she thought.

"How long does it last?" Pam asked.

Susan looked at her curiously. "How long does what last?"

"The night classes."

"Oh, that," Susan said. "I don't know. I think it's two nights a week for four weeks or something like that."

As they approached Susan's locker, Pam said, "I just figured it up. Your driver's ed class will be shorter than mine. You'll be finished sooner."

"So?"

"So nothing, I guess. You're probably going to take a condensed version. You've always been a whiz at everything else. Why not driver's ed?"

Susan stuffed her books into her locker and pulled out her history book that she'd left there overnight. "I'm pretty sure being a whiz in school has very little to do with driving. You can't think a car into a parallel parking space."

"I know. But you know how people think about smart kids."

"How do people think about smart kids?" Susan asked.

"They think they can do anything. I think you can do anything. Your mom thinks you can do anything, I bet. That's just the way it works."

"I think your reasoning is a little off base, Pam, but I don't—"

"Well, well, well," Pam interrupted. "Look who's here."

Susan turned and saw Roger and Jerry approaching. Her heart fluttered a little when Jerry smiled at her.

"Hi, Susan. How's it going?"

"Fine." Susan looked at Jerry as though

she were seeing him for the first time in a long time. He was the same Jerry Myers, of course. Still the tall lanky boy with the sandy blond hair that always looked windblown. And his pale blue eyes were still as blue. But things between them just seemed more distant than they did before classes started.

"I tried to call you last night, Pam," Roger said. "Where were you?"

Pam sighed. "My parents dragged me off to my grandmother's for dinner, then they stayed and stayed. You know how that goes."

"Yeah. Do I ever," Roger said.

"Did you want something special?" Pam asked. She cocked her eyebrow and toyed with a cluster of brown curls that covered her ear. "Or did you just want to talk?"

Roger smiled. "I wanted to know if you would like to go to the football game with me on Friday night."

"Are you serious?" Pam shouted. "I'd love to!"

Jerry shifted his weight from one foot to the other and glanced from the floor to the lockers and finally to Susan.

"Would you like to go with me, Susan?" he asked hesitantly. "I thought maybe we all could go together."

Susan stood there silent for a moment. A date? A real date? Clearing her throat, she finally said, "Yes. Sure. I'd like to go to the game with you."

"Great!" Roger said, taking charge of the situation. "I'll get all the plans worked out and let everybody know when we're leaving. Okay?"

"Sounds good to me," Pam said, glancing at her watch. "Now that that's settled, we'd better hit it. We've got to get to class."

Susan watched the three of them walk off together. It would have been so nice if I could have been in their classes, she thought. Somehow it just didn't seem right for Pam to be in Roger's class and Jerry's class, too.

Susan paused as she stepped into the history classroom. Her gaze locked on Gina standing beside her desk talking. I didn't know she knew him, Susan thought, gazing at the boy she hadn't been able to take her eyes off the day before. Boy, that Gina is sure different from what I thought. If finding a friend was her "first day of school plan," her "second day of school plan" must be to find a boyfriend. "I don't know where she got the idea that she was shy," Susan said to herself.

She walked to her seat and tried to fluff off the cloud of jealousy that had tried to settle on her. This is stupid, she thought. You can't be envious of Gina Tate over a boy you don't know, especially when you've been asked out on your first date by somebody you know and like a lot.

Susan couldn't help but feel as though she had broken up a party when she sat in her desk between Gina and the boy.

She glanced at him and he smiled at her. She felt her knees dissolve at the charm of his deep brown eyes. She took a deep breath. I can't let myself keep acting this way over you, she told herself, her gaze wandering in his direction. I've got Jerry. And you've got Gina. I guess. Besides, you're out of my league. Aren't you?

Susan went through her morning classes in a daze. Waiting in the cafeteria line behind Gina, she thought about how it was only the second day of school and already the assignments were getting tough. I'm already in a fog in that geometry class, she thought. I don't know if I'm going to be able to make the grades this year or not.

The line moved slowly and the noise in the large room was so loud that the only clear words Susan heard were those playing inside her head.

The testing next week and the week after isn't going to be easy, either, she told herself. What if I don't pass? Taking the tests and not passing. Being removed from gifted classes after you already had been placed there. That would be worse than being in them originally.

"There ought to be a law against scheduling biology after lunch," Gina said, picking up a tray in the line. "I can hardly work up an appetite when I know I'll soon be taking notes on a lecture about a frog's reproduction system."

Susan smiled. "I know what you mean."

The roar of a hundred voices talking at the same time surrounded them once again as they stepped out of the line and headed for an empty table.

Gina poked at the lettuce and tomato salad in front of her. "Are you going to take driver's ed this semester?"

Driver's ed again. "I think so."

"Me, too. I'm taking it in night school. I'm going to enroll in the class that starts tonight. What session are you going to take?"

Susan swallowed the bite of macaroni and cheese that she'd just popped into her mouth. "I haven't decided yet, but if you're taking the one tonight, I might do that, too."

"I wish you would." Gina grinned. "Seems as though we're doing everything together these days."

"You read my mind," Susan said. "I'll talk

to my mom about it and try to get over there and enroll in that class tonight."

Susan watched Gina glance around the cafeteria and wondered if she were simply taking in the sights of all the kids or if she might be looking for the boy who was in their three gifted classes.

"Who is that guy you were talking to this morning when I walked into first hour?" Susan asked suddenly.

"You mean the one who sits on the other side of you?"

"Yeah." Susan tried to keep from sounding too interested.

Gina smiled. "That's Neil Kellogg. He's new. Just moved next door to me about a month ago. He's super nice."

"Looks like a nice guy," Susan said, not knowing what to say now that she had brought him into the conversation.

"He is," Gina said. "We were just talking before class this morning about how strange it was that I'm really the only person he knows, and here we are in the first three classes of the day together." She raised her eyebrows. "He must be a brain."

"Like you," Susan laughed.

"Like you."

Susan moved the macaroni and cheese to the far corner of her tray and pulled a piece of chocolate cake forward to take its place. "So how does he like Castleview High?"

Gina shrugged her shoulders. "About like we do, I guess. We didn't have much time to talk this morning, and I didn't see him yesterday afternoon. Since he moved in, we've talked across the yard several times." Gina pushed her gold-framed glasses up on her nose. "He did say that he'd talked to Mr. Fleming about the Honor Society, and he's going to join that group. I have a feeling he's really smart. Know what I mean?"

"Yeah." Susan said. She played with the icing on the cake and wondered if he was too smart for her. For the first time in her life, she found herself wondering if she was smart enough to be around somebody. "Sounds like you and Neil have a good relationship going."

A pinkish tint came to Gina's cheeks. "There's no *relationship*," she said. "Heck, I wouldn't know a relationship if it knocked me down. I'm not interested in guys yet. Oh, you know what I mean. I like them for friends, but I'm not interested in dating yet. I know that boys like to tease, and I have a hard time with that." Gina took a sip of milk. "Even when my girlfriends tease me about my high grades."

Susan thought about the times Pam had teased her about being smart or about an *A* grade that she had made when the rest of the class made *B*'s and worse. "I know what you mean. Sometimes that teasing is hard to take. I've never been able to completely ignore it."

"Me either. I think that's why I've always been so shy about making friends. Seems like the closer your friends get to you, the more they tease you. It's just hard for me."

Susan stared at the redheaded girl with the gold-rimmed glasses across from her. She doesn't look anything like me on the outside, Susan thought. But she is a lot like me on the inside.

"I'll introduce you to Neil," Gina said suddenly, swallowing a bite of butterscotch pudding. "I know you two would like each other. Like I said, he's a nice guy, and since we're all in this gifted thing together, you might as well get to know him now." She smiled. "Besides, he may be the only one of us with the answers when we get into this stuff."

"Particularly geometry," Susan said. "I'm afraid that class is going to get me."

"I just wish he was in our biology class. I have the same feelings about it as you do geometry." Gina placed her napkin on her tray. "Oh, well, maybe these classes won't be too bad."

"Maybe not," Susan answered. What would it be like to be introduced to the cutest guy in Castleview High? In her mind, she answered her own question. "It will be too wonderful to imagine."

4

Susan had dinner on the table when her mother arrived home from work.

"What's this? Two nights in a row?" Patty Harris said.

"I've decided to take the driver's ed class that begins tonight," Susan said, placing two water glasses on the table. "It starts at six-thirty, and I'll have to get there a few minutes early to enroll." Susan took her place at the table and began to eat before her mother could be seated.

"Susan. Slow down," Patty said, smoothing the napkin across her lap. "You aren't going to a fire, you know. We'll get there in time."

Susan nodded and continued to attack the fried chicken and baked potato on her plate.

"What made you decide on the class tonight?" her mother asked. "I thought when we discussed it last night that you weren't sure what you were going to do."

"I wasn't, last night. I just decided today." Susan took a sip of water and then quickly began explaining the situation. "See. Gina Tate—she's in all of my classes except one—we weren't friends before—but we are this year—well, anyway . . ."

"Get on with it," Patty said, smiling. "We're going to be late just waiting for you to get this all out."

Susan grinned. "I'm trying to tell you. Gina Tate is a new friend of mine. She is taking the driver's ed class tonight, and so I decided I'd take it tonight, too, since I was going to take it anyway. That way, I will be in a class with somebody I know. See?"

"I see."

Susan sensed that her mother was going to start another one of her mini-speeches. "Don't get fired up," she said, grinning. "I know that it's okay to be an individual. I know that I have to think for myself, and I know that I don't *have* to have someone at my side every waking moment. I know all of that stuff." She stood and dramatically threw her napkin to the table. "And now, ta-da! We've got to get going. Gina's going to be waiting for me."

When Susan walked through the doors of Castleview High, she paused in the foyer and wondered if she would get enrolled by the time class started. So many people, she thought.

She made her way through the registration line, and just as she reached the registration table, she saw Gina in the line across from her.

"I thought I'd probably missed you," Susan said, trying to talk above the noise of the crowd.

"I saw you get in line. I was going to wait for you once I got enrolled."

Susan and Gina took their registration forms and moved away from the registration tables.

"Room one sixty-eight," Susan said. "This way."

"I'm right behind you," Gina said as they threaded their way through the congested hallway. "I sure am glad you decided to take this class tonight."

"Me, too," Susan said, glancing over her shoulder at Gina.

"Is Pam going to enroll tonight too?" Gina asked, walking beside Susan.

"No. She's going to take driver's ed before school. Most of my friends are," Susan said.

"I asked Angie to enroll tonight," Gina said. "You know. We've been friends for a long time. Almost all of junior high." Her voice lowered slightly. "But she didn't want to come tonight. Guess those tests we're going to take will make us the only sophomores at Castleview that aren't in morning driver's ed."

"I guess." Susan stopped in the center of the hallway and glanced at the door on her left. "My slip shows this to be the place," she said, holding her enrollment receipt in front of her face. "How about yours?"

"Same," Gina said as she walked into the room ahead of Susan. She headed for the window desks. It was easy to see why. Neil was seated at one of them. Sliding in behind Neil, Gina motioned for Susan to sit beside him. "Where were you this morning? Were you sick?" Gina asked Neil by way of greeting.

Susan's heart thundered in her ears. She had wondered herself why he had not been at school that morning. Enviously, she watched Gina talk to him as effortlessly as if he were her brother.

"I had to go to the dentist," Neil said. "I missed all of my morning classes."

"Nothing too serious, I hope."

"No. It was just a checkup. But the office was packed, and I had to wait so long to get in that when I finished, it wasn't really worth going back to school before lunch." He smiled at Gina. "History and English I could miss. It's geometry that's got me a little worried. How was it?"

"Not bad. I really don't see the problem with geometry. It's not as big a deal as you guys make it sound."

"You guys?" Neil asked. "Gina, check your glasses. There's only one of me sitting here. See?"

Gina's face pinked. "I know. I guess I was just thinking about you and Susan. She can't stand geometry."

Susan glanced at the ceiling. I wish I could disappear, she thought.

Gina shifted in her desk and smiled at Neil. "I'd like you to meet her." She pointed to Susan with her open palm. "Neil. My friend Susan Harris. Susan. My new neighbor, and friend, Neil Kellogg."

Neil grinned broadly. "Hi, Susan," he said. "It's nice to meet you. I've seen you in class. But I've been so busy trying to find my way around and learn the high school routine that I haven't taken time to introduce myself to you."

"I know what you mean," Susan said. "High school is a lot different from junior high. I'm having a bit of trouble adjusting myself."

Susan felt herself smiling inanely. She knew she was still smiling a few minutes later when the instructor walked into the room.

"It's six-thirty, and time to get started," he said, closing the door behind him as he entered. "My name is Lanny Townes, and I'll be your instructor for the next four weeks. As you can see, we're a small class," he said, nodding toward them as a group. "We will have four training cars, with three students in each of them."

Susan glanced at Neil and Gina. There're three of us, she thought. Three of us against nine adults. A shiver streaked through her. He just has to let us be in the same car.

Mr. Townes picked up some booklets on the corner of the desk. "I'm going to assign you to cars next week, and I'll have an assistant instructor helping me once we start driving." He held a booklet in the air. "These are the books you'll be studying from. Driving rules and regulations. One hour of each class will be spent in the classroom reviewing this material, and the other hour will be spent in the cars. This," he said, slapping the booklet in his hand, "is what you're going to need to know to pass your written test to get your driver's permit. And the actual driving practice is what you're going to need to eventually get your driver's license."

Susan listened intently, hoping that when the class was assigned to cars she and Gina would be together. She tried to tell herself that she didn't care whether or not Neil got in their car. If she could be with Gina, it would be all right.

When the class ended, Neil stood and turned to Gina. "Guess I'll see you two tomorrow." He glanced at Susan and smiled.

"Bright and early," Gina said. "After all. You've got two days' work to do."

As they filed out of the classroom, Neil said, "Hey. If you don't mind, can I call you in a little while after you get home and get those assignments we're supposed to do for tomorrow? I've got all of my books at the house."

"Sure," Gina said. "That would be fine. The only thing we had was your favorite. Geometry."

Neil smiled at Gina. "I bet you've already completed the assignment, haven't you?"

"I've finished it. It isn't hard," Gina said.

"Don't let her fool you," Susan said. "I looked at it before I came over here this evening. It's hard."

Neil smiled at her. "My kind of person."

They stopped outside the classroom door.

"See you girls at the same place tomorrow," Neil said casually. He waved and walked down the hall toward the back entrance of the building.

"I guess I'll follow him," Gina said. "I told my mom to pick me up in the back oval instead of the front."

"I told my mom the front." Susan turned away from Gina and started for the foyer. "Thanks for talking me into this. I think it's going to be fun."

"I think so, too," Gina said. "See you tomorrow."

Susan walked out of the building into the cool, damp air. She glanced up at the full moon that hid behind the large fanned leaves of the palm trees lining the school's drive. I'm not going to fight that geometry tonight, she thought. I can probably do it in school tomorrow.

"What a morning." Susan sighed, placing her lunch tray on the table beside Gina's. "Who would have thought that things would be so rugged on the third day of school? In junior high, nobody really got serious about studying until the second or third *week* of school."

"For sure." Gina pulled her chair closer to the table and began arranging the plates and bowls on her tray. "History was kind of fun. I'm looking forward to that Honor Society meeting Friday. I think Mr. Fleming is probably my favorite teacher."

"Mine, too," Susan said. "He's sure better than Mrs. Staley. I tell you what, she's just not getting through to me. I didn't even turn in last night's assignment."

"You didn't?" Gina placed her fork on the side of her plate and stared at Susan. "That geometry assignment wasn't really that hard. If you couldn't do it, why didn't you call me?"

"Oh, I don't know. I had planned to do it after our class last night, but I didn't. I'm sure I can do it. I'll give it another shot tonight. I don't have anything planned for this evening and I can spend some time with it."

"With it and tonight's assignment, too."

"Don't remind me," Susan said.

"Mind if I join you?" a voice behind Susan asked.

Susan turned. It was Pam. "Of course I don't mind. Have a seat," she said, pulling out a chair for Pam beside her own chair.

"I saw you two come out of the line together."

"You two remember each other from junior high, don't you?" Susan said, feeling strangely uncomfortable between them.

"Sure. Hi, Pam," Gina said.

"Hi," Pam said.

Susan glanced at Pam, waiting for her to say something more. A smile was frozen on her lips, and Susan thought it was the most saccharine smile she'd ever seen.

"Roger and Jerry and I are all signed up for driver's ed," Pam said, opening her carton of milk. "It's going to be so much fun. Starts next Monday, you know." She took a sip of the milk, then added, "It's really too bad that you can't be in our class."

"I bet you'll have a good time," Gina said. "We really did last night, didn't we, Susan?"

Pam glared at Susan.

Before Susan could respond, Gina said, "Oh, didn't you tell Pam that we enrolled in that class last night?"

"No," Susan said. She glanced at Pam. "I haven't seen her often enough lately to tell her about it." She turned her attention back to her lunch, then said, "It was a spur-of-the-moment decision, anyway."

"Well, our first class was last night, Pam," Gina said. "If yours is anything like ours, I bet you'll really like it."

"I'm sure I'll like it fine," Pam said. "I remember now that you did say that you couldn't be in our class, Susan, and that you'd probably take something at night." An accusing stare returned to her eyes. "Why didn't you tell me that you were enrolling so soon?"

"I would have if I had seen you," Susan said, matching Pam's accusing stare with one of her own. "I would have told you lots of things if I had seen you. Where have you been hiding? I've planned to ride home on the bus with you for the past two days, and you haven't been on it. And this morning, you didn't want a ride to school, so I couldn't talk to you then, either."

"Get hold of yourself," Pam said to Susan. "That was no big deal. I haven't been riding the bus, and I didn't ride with you this morning because I've been riding with Roger and his brother, Tommy."

Susan frowned. "Tommy? I thought he graduated last year."

"No. He graduates this year. And he has a

car and so I've been riding with them." Pam toyed with the food on her tray. "We thought Tommy was going to take us all to the football game on Friday, but he has a date, and he doesn't think we can all crowd into his car." Pam winked. "At least that's the excuse he's giving Roger. If you know what I mean."

"Uh, yes," Susan stammered. Her heart beat faster. The football game. Her date with Jerry. How could she have forgotten to ask her mother about that?

"You can go with us, can't you?" Pam asked. "I mean, Jerry asked you out. You did talk to your mom about it, didn't you?"

Before Susan could answer, Gina scooted her chair away from the table and stood.

"I've got to run, Susan. I'll see you in biology." Gina picked up her tray and walked away from the table without saying another word to either Pam or Susan.

"What's her problem?" Pam asked.

Susan paused. "She's having a hard time with biology. I'm sure she just wanted to get to class and get in a few extra minutes of study time before class started," she said.

"You brains don't need extra study time. Who you trying to kid?" Pam popped bites of food into her mouth between speeches. "I've known who Gina Tate was ever since we were in elementary school. When I was sitting at my desk waiting for the blue group to be called to the reading circle, I spent a lot of time staring at the backs of you greens. Gina was one of them."

Susan thought of her own problems in geometry. "Sometimes things aren't as easy as they seem."

"Maybe not," Pam said. "Can you go?"

"Where?"

"To the game." Pam sighed and took a long sip of her milk. "Good grief. Where are you, Susan?" She stared straight into Susan's eyes. "Are you in there? Yoooooo. Are you in there?"

"Of course I'm in here. You're babbling again, in case you haven't noticed."

Pam started to laugh. "I've missed you, Susan. Where have you been for the past few days?"

"Pam!" Susan grinned.

"I know, I know. I'm the one who's been gone. So, tell me what your mom said about our date."

What my mom said, Susan thought. What would my mom have said if I had asked her?

"She said that it probably would be okay, but she wants to think about it for a little while and she will let me know something for sure this evening," Susan lied. "You know how my mom is."

"Yeah. About like mine," Pam said. "Well, my mom gave the okay immediately, so yours probably will, too."

"Probably," Susan said evasively.

Pam scooted her dishes to one side of her tray and pulled the bowl of chocolate pudding toward her. "That Gina is weird, isn't she? How'd you ever get stuck with her?"

"She isn't as weird as we used to think," Susan said defensively. "And I didn't really get stuck with her. I guess you could say that we chose each other. She's the only person in my homeroom that's in most of my classes. She's in all but one."

"Lucky you."

"I am lucky. How would you like to go around all day without someone to talk to or have lunch with?" Susan folded her hands across the edge of her tray. "Besides, Gina's kind of shy and doesn't make friends as easily as you do."

"I'm shy, too," Pam said innocently.

"You don't have a shy bone in your body," Susan said. She grinned. "Sly, yes. But shy? No."

"Why, whatever do you mean?"

"You know," Susan said. "If you weren't a

little bit sly, you wouldn't have Roger wrapped around your little finger."

Pam inhaled the last bite of her pudding. "It is wonderful, isn't it? Things are going so great for us. He's been coming over every night, and I really think that before long, he's going to ask me to go with him." Pam's brown eyes widened and her eyebrows disappeared into the mound of tight curls resting on her forehead. "You know, I bet he asks me at the game on Friday night. Or maybe after the game," she said excitedly, as though the thought was new to her at that moment. "It'll be so much fun. His dad is going to drop us off at the stadium, and after the game, we are going to walk across the street to the Burger Brigade. We can stay as long as we want to—"

"Or until my mom tells me I have to be in," Susan interrupted.

"Or until you have to be in. Then all we have to do is call Roger's dad, and he'll pick us up at the Brigade and take us home." Pam's brown eyes sparkled. "Won't it be wonderful when we get out of these driver's ed classes and can drive ourselves to the games, or for hamburgers, or whatever we want to do?" She clasped her hands in front of her. "It will be terrific. I can hardly wait."

5

When Susan walked into class on Thursday morning, the world seemed a brighter place than it had been the afternoon before. Her mother had given the okay for her to go out with Jerry, Pam and Roger on Friday night, even though she had been hesitant at first. I'm a little hesitant, too, Susan thought, taking her seat. First-date jitters, I guess.

While she waited for Gina and Neil to appear, Susan thought about Pam and her phone call last night. A warm pleasant feeling flowed through her as she remembered how excited Pam was and how things seemed to be just the way they had been during the summer.

Susan placed her history book on the top of her desk and was pleased with the way her homework assignment from the night before had turned out. She'd dreaded these special classes partially because they set her apart from her friends, and partially because she wondered if she could make the grades she was accustomed to making. So far, so good, she thought, taking the homework assignment from her notebook. You're hanging in there, kid. In this class, anyway.

With only a couple of seconds to spare before class began, Gina and Neil hurriedly entered the classroom. Both had time to say hi to Susan but nothing else.

"Our morning bulletin today is short," Mr. Fleming said as soon as the bell sounded. "But I think it will be of special interest to this class." He took his place at the front of the classroom and glanced at the paper in his hand, then back at the class. "The Honor Society meeting tomorrow afternoon will be extended an extra half hour to honor the students in the new gifted program at Castleview High." Mr. Fleming looked at them and smiled. "You people." He glanced back at the paper. "The business meeting will include introduction of new members, and the society will plan its activities and projects for the coming year." Placing the bulletin on the corner of his desk, he said, "The meeting will be in the cafeteria. Three o'clock to five."

When the bell rang for dismissal, Gina grabbed Susan's arm before she could gather her books. "Isn't it great?" Gina said excitedly.

"Isn't what great? That we have to read chapter four and do the review questions for tomorrow?" Susan asked, thinking of Mr. Fleming's final words.

"No, silly. The Honor Society meeting and the little reception they're holding for us after the meeting. I think it's terrific." Gina glanced at Neil as he started to leave. "You're going to the Honor Society meeting tomorrow, aren't you, Neil?"

"Sure am."

"You're going, too, aren't you, Susan?" Gina asked.

"Of course," Susan said, without thinking.

"Good. We can go together, and my mom can take you home."

"Fine," Susan said, trying to keep her thoughts from scattering. There's the Honor Society meeting, the reception, the football game tomorrow night with the gang and driver's ed tonight. And there'll be homework. There's always homework, she thought worriedly.

Susan traveled from class to class and felt as though the day would never end. By the time she got home from school and worked on her geometry assignment for a while, it was past time to begin dinner.

She and her mother grabbed a quick sandwich for dinner, and then it was back to school again for Susan's driver's education class that evening.

"I'm beginning to feel like I'm on a roller coaster," Susan said, collapsing in the desk across from Gina. "I barely had time to get some homework done and then get back over here."

"I know what you mean," Gina said. "I'm afraid that Tuesday and Thursday nights are going to be pretty hectic for the next four weeks."

"That's not going to do us a bit of good when we have to take those aptitude tests at seven in the morning on Monday, Wednesday and Friday for the next two weeks."

"For sure," Gina agreed.

Susan waited for the class to begin. From time to time she glanced at Neil's empty desk. I'd like to get to know him better, she thought, but where will I ever find the time?

Finally Neil appeared and took his seat in front of Gina. Gina's lucky, Susan thought.

She lives right next door to Neil. She probably sees him every day. . . .

Shortly after the class began, the moment Susan had been both looking forward to and dreading arrived: the assignment of students to cars.

"The easiest way to do this is alphabetically," Mr. Townes said, taking an enrollment list from the top of his desk. "When I call your name, make a note as to which car you're in. We'll be working with the cars later in this class period."

Immediately, Susan knew that she and Gina wouldn't be in the same car. Harris and Tate were too far apart. Probably none of us will be together, Susan thought, as Mr. Townes began calling names.

"Arrington, Baker and Giles. Car number one," Mr. Townes said. "Car number two. Harris, Johnson and Kellogg."

Kellogg! Susan thought. We are going to be in the same car? She shifted in her desk and her thoughts raced so rapidly that she missed the names in car three. She barely regained her composure in time to hear Mr. Townes call out car four.

"Tate, Wilson and Yardley."

Poor Gina, Susan thought. She will be with two strangers.

Susan paid little attention to the lecture

Mr. Townes gave. She spent most of the hour thinking about how it was going to be to have driver's training with Neil.

The class marched in mass outside to the parking lot after the lecture, and Mr. Townes pointed out the cars.

"Car-number-one group here," he said, pointing to a new sedan to his right. "Car two, here. Three, and four," he said, pointing as he spoke.

Susan glanced at Neil and grinned, following him to the new car that had been designated as number two. They waited beside the car and watched a woman who appeared to be almost fifty approaching the car.

"She must be the Johnson he called out," Neil whispered.

"I guess so," Susan said. She watched the woman closely. "I wonder why she hasn't learned to drive before now?"

"Who knows? I wonder why most of these people haven't learned to drive before now."

Mr. Townes assigned other assistant instructors to each of the cars before walking over to Susan's and Neil's car.

"You can go ahead and get in," he said, opening the front door for the older woman.

"I . . . I don't want to be first," she stammered, visibly shaken by the thought of being the first one of the group to drive the car.

Susan and Neil climbed into the back seat while Mr. Townes persuaded the woman to get into the car.

"None of you has driven before, I assume," Mr. Townes said, trying to reason with her. "And each of you will be a little nervous about it at first."

Mrs. Johnson seated herself behind the steering wheel and closed the door.

"The first thing you all will do before ever starting the engine is adjust the seat so that it's comfortable for you," Mr. Townes said. "Check the distance between you and the steering wheel, and be sure the brake and accelerator pedals are within easy reach." He waited for Mrs. Johnson to adjust her seat, and then he continued. "The next thing you'll do is adjust your mirrors." He pointed to the rearview mirror and the accent mirror on the driver's side of the car. "It's important to adjust these each time you change your seat position so you can clearly see the cars behind and to the side of your vehicle."

Mr. Townes told them about the knobs and switches and what each of the warning lights meant, referring the three students to their manuals for additional information. "Let me emphasize one thing. And I can't emphasize it enough, really," he said. "Be sure to read and study your manuals thoroughly. Remember this: The written test is just as important in obtaining a driver's license as the driving test itself.''

Susan looked at Neil and he looked at her and raised his eyebrows. She wondered if he was thinking the same thing she was thinking: How could anything be as important as the driving test?

Mr. Townes instructed Mrs. Johnson on starting the car; then he had her pull forward and put the car in reverse, then in the drive position again.

The woman jerked the car into gear and forgot to hold her foot on the brake each time, even though Mr. Townes reminded her to hold her foot there every time she changed gears.

I may not get out of here alive, Susan thought, lurching with every move Mrs. Johnson forced the car to make. This woman may kill me before this course is over.

Susan was relieved when Mrs. Johnson's turn at driving was over. Her relief was short-lived, though, when she heard Mr. Townes say, "Susan. Why don't you change places with Ramona now?"

Susan got out of the car and slid behind the wheel as Ramona Johnson scooted across the back seat. The look in Mrs. Johnson's eyes told Susan that she was thrilled to be out of the driver's seat.

Please don't mess up, Susan said to herself. Don't do something totally stupid.

She listened to Mr. Townes repeat his instructions and carefully tried to keep her foot on the brake while changing gears. Here goes, she thought, the car in drive and her foot firmly on the brake pedal. She gently lifted her foot from the brake and pressed the accelerator. When she touched her toe to the accelerator, nothing happened.

"You'll have to touch it a little harder than that," Mr. Townes said, smiling.

Susan pushed the long pedal with her toes and the car lunged forward. Then, startled by the quick forward motion, Susan lifted her foot from the accelerator and hit the brake pedal, causing the car to jerk to a halt.

Her cheeks burned with embarrassment. She wished that Neil had been second, and that she had been last. Now I know how poor Mrs. Johnson felt, she thought, considerably more sympathetic now that she was in the driver's seat.

"That's all right," Mr. Townes assured her as he had done for Mrs. Johnson. "As you can see, driving isn't as easy as it looks. And beginning is one of the hardest parts. It just takes a little time to get the feel of the car and build a little confidence in yourself."

As if Susan didn't feel bad enough about her performance, she really felt bad when Neil got his turn behind the wheel. It was almost as if he had driven before. His moves were all so smooth. He hardly jerked or lunged at all.

By the time Neil had finished, Susan had assured herself that Neil's near-perfect performance was the result of listening to Mr. Townes point out hers and Mrs. Johnson's mistakes. He knew what to watch for, she told herself.

"Now you all can practice these things we've gone over tonight if you want to," Mr. Townes said, after Neil placed the car in park and turned off the ignition switch. "As a matter of fact, you could get together and practice if you wanted. I think there's some advantage to learning from each other's accomplishments and mistakes." He smiled at them collectively. "But if you practice, do it in your driveway or have your parents bring you over here to the school parking lot," he said looking at Susan and Neil. "You all aren't ready for street driving yet. That will come later."

Mr. Townes dismissed them, and Susan got out of the car trying to imagine herself getting together with Ramona Johnson to practice. "No way," her thoughts kept saying. "No way."

"No way for sure," she mumbled, walking toward the car Gina was standing beside.

"Did you say something?"

Surprised that anyone was close enough to her to hear, Susan turned and saw Neil smiling at her.

"Oh, no, I . . . I was just talking to myself," Susan said. "I just thought I did such a terrible job of this that I'll probably never learn to drive. I was just scolding myself for doing such a lousy job."

Neil shrugged his broad shoulders. "Heck, I thought you did a good job for the first time out."

"Not as good as yours."

A sly grin stole across his lips. "Yeah. But I cheated," Neil admitted. "My dad's taken me out to the driving strip north of town a couple of times and I've had a little practice at this part already."

"No wonder you knew what you were doing!" Susan shouted.

Gina walked over to join them. "What's this all about?"

"Neil cheated on his driving lesson," Susan said.

Neil explained the whole thing to Gina.

"Well, all I've got to say is that for three people who are enrolled in gifted classes, we're a mess when it comes to driving," Gina said.

6

Susan had mixed emotions as she walked into the school cafeteria for the Honor Society meeting and reception. She knew that attending this meeting was the thing to do. After all, it was more than just a club meeting. Mr. Fleming had told them that some of the things the Honor Society was going to be doing this year could be used to apply toward their grade in history. Even Mrs. Winters, their English teacher, had told them that they could make written reports on the Honor Society projects and receive extra credit in her class for their participation in the Society.

If I could get extra credit in geometry for

94

this, Susan thought, taking a seat at one of the front tables so that Gina could easily find her, I'd have it made.

Susan glanced around the room at the people filing in, and for the first time all week she was glad that Pam didn't ride home with her on the bus anymore. She probably wouldn't understand why I came to this meeting, Susan thought. And I'm not sure I could explain why.

Susan kept her gaze locked on the door, and soon Gina entered the room, with Neil right behind her. For someone who doesn't like boys, she's with him all the time. Or maybe he's with her?

"Been waiting long?" Gina asked, sitting beside Susan.

"No. I just got here."

"Looks like we just got here in time ourselves," Neil said, nodding to Mr. Fleming, who was taking his place at the front of the room.

Mr. Fleming waited for a moment until all talking ceased. "I'd like to welcome all of you Castleview High's Honor Society. For you returning members, we are glad to see you back. We are proud of your past accomplishments in the Society, and we are looking forward to your leadership this coming year." Mr. Fleming smiled that thin smile that had become so familiar to Susan over the past week. "And, to you new members, and guests, we welcome you. We hope that you will join us, will be active members in our group, and we look forward to your input and new ideas. New ideas and experienced leadership. Those are the elements that have made this group one of the outstanding organizations at Castleview High. And, as your sponsor, let me say that I am looking forward to another year of working with you exceptional people."

"He's laying it on pretty strong, isn't he?" Gina whispered.

Susan nodded, afraid to say anything for fear that her voice would carry through the stillness and reach Mr. Fleming.

"I think before we get started we should all take a moment to get to know each other. Let's start here," he said, pointing at a girl on the front row, "and introduce yourself and tell what grade you're in and a little bit about yourself."

Each person had a turn. When it was Susan's turn, she stood and simply said, "I'm Susan Harris. Mr. Fleming's homeroom."

After the introductions, Mr. Fleming said, "Well, as you can see, we have an excellent group." He shuffled some papers on the table beside him and moved one from the middle of the stack to the top. "The first order of business is to nominate our officers for the new year." That thin smile returned to his lips. "For you new people, we have a president, a vice-president and a secretary. And, in an attempt to be fair and maintain our established leadership, our president must be a senior who has been an Honor Society member all three years. Our vice-president must be a junior, with the same stipulation, and our secretary is a sophomore in good standing. With those qualifications in mind, let's open the nominations for secretary."

Susan glanced around the room and saw a few of the people in her homeroom and first-hour history class. Almost without thinking, she raised her hand in the air.

"Yes, Susan."

"Mr. Fleming. I'd like to nominate Gina Tate for secretary."

Gina turned to Susan, her eyes wide. She clenched her teeth and forced the words between them. "Are you crazy?"

Susan turned away from her and tried to ignore her.

"We have one nomination for secretary. Miss Gina Tate. Stand up, Gina, so that everyone will know who you are."

Gina slowly stood and rapidly took her seat again.

"Mr. Fleming," Neil said, hand in the air. "I'd like to make a motion that we nominate Gina Tate as Honor Society secretary by acclamation."

"I second the motion," a fellow classmate shouted from the back of the room.

"I'll get you for this," Gina whispered, leaning toward Susan.

"The motion has been made and seconded that we nominate Miss Gina Tate as secretary," Mr. Fleming said. "All in favor, say aye." He paused for a moment. "Opposed, no." The thin smiled traveled across his face and off again. "Gina. You're our new secretary. Come up here and take a seat."

Gina rose from her chair and seated herself at the table facing the group.

The other elections went as rapidly as the one for secretary, and once they were over, Mr. Fleming turned the meeting over to the new president, Bob Baker, a tall, thin boy who, Mr. Fleming said, had carried a four-point average every semester he'd been at Castleview.

"The first order of business," Bob said, "is the call for project and activity ideas for the coming year, from the floor." He glanced around the room. "Do I hear a recommendation?"

The room was quiet. Finally, Neil raised his hand.

"Mr. President. I don't have a recommendation to make just yet. I would like some clarification, though."

Bob nodded to Neil. "And you are?"

"Neil Kellogg. I am new to this community, and I feel that I am really at a loss as to what the Society has done in the past." Neil shifted his weight to the other foot. "That's what I need clarification on. I'd like to know if you limit your activities to the Castleview High district, or if you are open to projects that would include the Matanzas Bay area?"

Bob glanced at Mr. Fleming, and then back at Neil. "We have usually stayed within the Castleview High district," he said. "But I see no reason why we couldn't expand." He glanced at Mr. Fleming again. "Would you like to make a comment here, sir?"

"What have you got in mind, Neil?" Mr. Fleming asked.

"Well, I'm not sure, exactly. I guess I'm just brainstorming a little." Neil slipped his fingertips into his pockets and then removed them again as he began to speak. "As I said, I'm new to this community. I'm new to Florida, as a matter of fact." He smiled and folded his arms across his chest. "And, because I'm new here, I think I might look at the community a little differently from some of you."

Mr. Fleming raised his eyebrows and nodded. "Go on. I think you may be right."

"As I said, I'm just brainstorming, but I am intrigued with what we've got here at our fingertips. Just a few miles from here, we have St. Augustine, known as the oldest city in the United States. I haven't had much time to spend over there since we moved here, but I know it is loaded with history and things to see and report on. I came here as a tourist myself before we moved here. Why, the old fort alone is probably something that could be worked into a project."

"The Castillo de San Marcos is an interesting piece of history," Mr. Fleming said. "How would you work it into a project for our group?"

Susan's heart quickened. She knew Neil was on to something. She could feel his excitement and it stirred something in her.

"I don't have a handle on that yet," Neil said. He shrugged his shoulders. "I just think that since we have St. Augustine at our back door, we could use its history some way as a project and at the same time use the project and reports we might make on it as extra credit assignments in some of our classes."

Neil put his palms in the air, then let his hands fall to his side as he sat down. "I don't know. That's my thought."

"I think it's a good one," Bob said. He turned to Mr. Fleming and said, "Do you think there is something here that we could pursue?"

Mr. Fleming nodded. "I think Neil knows where he wants to go with this, or will know with a little bit of investigative work." He glanced over the room. "If you don't mind, Mr. President, I'd like to recommend that we appoint a committee of Neil and one or two other people to make a visit to St. Augustine. Look around. See what's to see, and what might work as a project for the group."

"You've heard Neil's idea and Mr. Fleming's recommendation. Do I have any volunteers to be on this committee with Neil to develop this project?" Bob asked.

Gina instantly raised her hand. "Mr. President."

"Yes. Gina."

"I think that because Neil is new to the community, the other person on the committee should be someone who has lived here all of his or her life. That would be a good balance, I think." She pushed her gold-rimmed glasses up on her nose and toyed with the pencil in her hand. "Susan Harris

would be a great person to be on this committee with Neil. She's lived here forever and
has spent a lot of time in St. Augustine over
the years."

"Susan, would you help on this committee?" Bob asked.

She nodded. "Sure, I'd be happy to,"
Susan said.

"Unless somebody else really wants to,"
Gina said, "I don't see any reason to have
more people on this committee. The ones
we've chosen will do a fine job, I'm sure."

"Do I have any more volunteers?" Bob
asked. When no one spoke, he glanced at
Neil and Susan. "Great. Why don't you two
get together, and when you've had time to
evaluate the possibilities, you can report
back to us at the next meeting, which will be
a dinner meeting."

Neil smiled at Susan and nodded in Bob's
direction. "We'll do it."

The rest of the business meeting was a blur
for Susan. She tried to concentrate on the
discussions, but all she could think about was
being on that committee with Neil, going
with him to St. Augustine and developing a
project for the group.

When the meeting ended, she stood and
walked toward Gina, who had already head-

ed for the punch bowl on the far side of the room.

"Thanks a lot," Susan said, standing at Gina's back as the girl poured a glass of punch. "Are you crazy?"

"You're welcome." Gina picked up a cookie. "And no, I'm not crazy. I told you I'd get you when you made me secretary." Taking a bite out of the cookie, she said, "Guess I got you."

"But you'll be perfect for the job," Susan said, pouring a glass of punch for herself. "That's—"

"And you'll be perfect for this committee." Gina glanced around them and then moved in closer to Susan. "I know you're crazy about Neil, Susan. Here's your chance to be with him. Legally." Gina smoothed a strand of red hair away from her glasses. "It's not a date, but it's a start."

"But I . . . I don't understand." Susan looked at Gina in disbelief. "How did you know I liked Neil? I haven't said that much about him. No more than anybody else would."

"I won't tell you that it's written all over your face, because I know you'll die. It's not, anyway. It's just that we've gotten to be pretty good friends. At least, I think we are, and good friends know stuff about good friends. I know you like Neil a lot. I think he likes you."

Susan sipped her punch and stared at Gina over the rim of her glass. He doesn't like me, she thought. Not the way I like him, anyway. I'm sure of that. "I like Neil as a friend. Let's just leave it at that," she said. "I'm sure that's the way he likes me. Okay?"

"Okay. Whatever you say."

"Whatever you say about what?" Neil said, walking up behind them.

Susan let out a small gasp and fumbled with the punch as she tried to regain her composure. She glanced at the clock on the wall across from them. "I was just telling Gina that I needed to be going soon. I've got a million things to do this evening, and Gina's mom is taking me home."

Gina nodded. "Gotcha." She set her cup on the table and said, "I'm waiting for you."

Susan smiled a good-bye at Neil, and as she turned away, he took her arm.

"When do you want to get together, 'committee member,' and go over to St. Augustine?"

Susan's heart raced at the thought. "Anytime you want to will probably be all right. We can't go on Sunday, because some of the stuff will be shut down. I think any Saturday would be okay." She hesitated before she finished her thought. "We probably should go early. That way we'd have all day if we needed it."

"I agree," Neil said. "How about tomorrow?"

Susan swallowed hard. Tomorrow? "Well, I think that would be okay," she said. "I'll need to check with my mother, though, and be sure that we don't have any plans made."

"Oh, sure. I know. I need to check with my folks, too. If everything's clear, though, I'll have my dad take us over there and pick us up at a certain time. Or we can call him. Whatever."

"That sounds fine," Susan said.

Gina cleared her throat and pointed to the clock. "My mom is going to come in here after us if we don't get out to the car," she teased.

"Okay. I'm ready," Susan said. She followed Gina away from the refreshment table, then paused as Neil called to her.

"Susan. Wait a second." He hurried to her. "How about giving me your phone number so I can call you tonight and check to be sure everything's set."

"Call me?" If he called, she would be out with Jerry and her mother might tell him. Susan dug through her purse looking for a pencil and paper as she thought about what to do next. She placed a scrap of paper on her purse and wrote her number on it. Under the number, she wrote *call before seven*. "Here we are," she said, handing the paper to Neil. "My mother and I will be gone this evening, but I will be able to let you know if you can call before seven."

"Okay. Talk to you then," Neil said, smiling.

7

Susan drifted through the evening on a cloud of daydreams. Her mother had given her permission to spend the following day in St. Augustine with Neil, and within the next hour he'd be calling her to be sure she could go. She glided around the room, alternating from being excited about Neil to being excited about being with Pam and Roger and Jerry again.

"If only Neil would ask me out someday," she said aloud. Before the thought could grow in her head, she blocked it with a simple, "Stop it!"

She slipped on a pair of jeans and a pale

yellow knit shirt. She pulled her long golden hair out from under the shirt, then slipped on a pair of tennis shoes. Taking a quick glance at herself in the mirror, she felt as though she should be dressed more spectacularly for her first date. But she decided that everyone else would be wearing the same thing she was. You don't get dressed up in heels for a football game, she told herself.

Susan walked into the living room to wait for Neil's call before her friends arrived. The minutes seemed like hours, and when she heard a car outside, and then the knock on the door, she knew that Neil was not going to find her there.

"He's late, anyway," she said, walking past the clock on the living room wall. "I said to call before seven. It's seven-thirty now."

Susan opened the door and saw Jerry smiling at her. He smiled broadly as their eyes met.

"Are you ready?"

"I'll be right there," Susan said. She needed to talk to her mother before she left. She had to talk to her, though, without Jerry listening. "I need to tell my mom that I'm leaving now," Susan said. "Why don't you go ahead and get in the car, and I'll be right out?"

Jerry nodded. Susan thought he looked

somewhat awkward standing on her front porch.

A first date, Susan thought, closing the door. What do you do, how do you act, what do you talk about on a first date?

She walked into the bedroom that her mother used to paint in. "I'm leaving now, Mom."

Patty Harris shifted her paintbrush to her left hand and pulled up the sleeve of the paint-splattered white sweatshirt. "Okay. Have a good time. And be home by midnight."

"I will," Susan said. She paused. "Mom. I was expecting Neil to call about tomorrow, and he hasn't."

"That's okay. When he calls, I'll tell him that you can go, and I'll ask him what time you should be ready." Smiling, Mrs. Harris picked up her paintbrush again. "Now, you better go on. Your friends are going to wonder if you are going to this football game with them or not."

Susan rushed out of the bedroom and hurried for the front door. "Thanks, Mom. See you around midnight."

Susan watched the clock tick off the final seconds of the game, then joined the other fans in the stands as they counted, "Ten, nine, eight, seven, six, five, four, three, two, one . . ."

Susan fell against Jerry as Pam jumped up and down and twirled in the stands at the Castleview Pirates' victory.

"That was so excellent," Pam shouted. "Didn't you just love that touchdown there in the last sixty seconds of the game? I loved it, I loved it," she said, clapping her hands. "We got one point up on them, and they didn't have time to pull out another play."

"Those guys definitely know how to throw that football," Roger said, taking Pam's arm. "I'm glad we've got a good team."

As they all filed out of the stands, Pam opened her purse. "Here. Wait a minute. We've got to wear these." She pulled four black eye patches out of her purse and gave one to each of them. "I bought these after the pep assembly today, and just now thought about them."

"Ding. We could have been wearing them during the game," Roger said.

"But if we'd worn them at the game, it would have been only half as good, since we would have been watching with only one eye."

That sounded like typical Pam Edwards logic, Susan thought. Leave it to Pam to always take something totally ridiculous and turn it around so that you are the one who thinks that there is a flaw in your thinking, not hers.

"Everybody put them on now," Pam said. "We can walk out of here and go across the street to the Burger Brigade, and everybody will know we're one of the Pirates and that we are part of the winning team."

Each of them slipped a patch over one eye. Susan fought her long hair as she tried to get the black patch to fit just right. Once in place, she began walking across the long rows of bleachers with Jerry following close behind her.

The patch over her eye disturbed her depth perception. As she took a step to the bleacher below her, Susan's foot touched the side of the stand and she felt herself falling forward.

She screamed and tried to catch herself to break the fall, then felt someone grab her arm, stopping her. She pulled the patch off her eye and looked over her shoulder to see that Jerry was holding her in his arms.

"You okay?" he asked, releasing his hold on her. He rubbed his hands along the sides of his jeans. "You . . . you didn't get hurt or anything, did you?"

"No, I'm not hurt," Susan said. "Just embarrassed."

"You should have been more careful," Pam said, her patch still in place. "You could have fallen into me and Roger."

Susan frowned. Fallen into her and Roger? I could have killed myself, she thought. "I'll be more careful the next time I decide to fall."

Pam and Roger led the way out of the stands onto the sidewalk that circled the stadium.

"We better hurry and get over to the Burger Brigade before all of the good tables are taken," Pam said.

"We better hurry before *all* of the tables are taken," Roger added.

Roger took Pam's hand and they almost jogged along the sidewalk toward the street that bordered the far end of the field.

Susan turned and saw Jerry right behind her and felt herself waiting for him to take her hand. She knew she shouldn't expect it. Why should she? They were just good friends. Pam and Roger were almost going together. There was a difference, and Susan knew it.

Susan's ankle hurt, and she couldn't keep up with Pam. "You go ahead if you want," she said, glancing at Jerry. She rubbed her ankle. "I can't go any faster. I really hurt myself back there."

Jerry looked at her and then looked at Pam and Roger, who were about ready to cross the street.

Susan could tell by the look in his eyes that he wanted to go ahead and be with them but felt as though he should stay there with her.

"I'll stay," he said reluctantly. "They can save us a table."

Susan walked slowly along the sidewalk and then made herself hurry across the street. It was late. Ten-thirty, and the traffic would have been light had it not been for the kids leaving the stadium, and the parents who had just arrived to pick up their sons or daughters who didn't drive.

Susan thought about how wonderful it was going to be when she finally got her driver's license. She wouldn't have a car of her own. But on nights like tonight, when her mother was just going to be at home painting, she could take the car and go wherever she needed or wanted to go. The feeling of freedom that the thought stirred in her was as invigorating as the cool, damp, night air.

When Susan and Jerry entered the Burger Brigade, they waited inside the door and peered through the darkened room for Pam and Roger.

"You see them?" Jerry asked.

"Not yet." Susan strained her neck to see them, feeling as though the loud music on the jukebox was a detriment to her vision. "There they are!" she said, pointing to Pam's waving arms in the far corner of the room. "Back there. In that round corner booth."

"It took you guys long enough to cross the street," Pam said. "What were you doing? Making out along the way since you'd gotten rid of us?"

Susan felt her face turning crimson, and she was glad the lights were low. Making out? She glanced at Jerry and shook her head. "I hurt my ankle when I fell, Pam. I couldn't walk any faster."

"Well, we got to the street and turned around and you two weren't there. How'd I know?"

"If you'd told us you were going to try to make it here in time that would break the record for the quarter mile, we would have told you what my problem was."

Roger folded his hand over Pam's and rested them both on the table. "Take the knife out of your mouth, little Pirate, and let's get serious about ordering some grub." He smiled at her and placed his forehead on hers. "I think we can get rid of the patches now, matie. This is another one of those two-eye deals you were talking about." He took off his patch and placed it on the table.

Pam removed the patch from her eye and placed it on the table beside Roger's. "I guess you're right." She took the patch that Jerry slid across the table and added it to the stack. Then, turning to Roger, she grinned. "Bring on the grub."

"Yeah, let's eat," Susan said. "I don't want to be the one to throw cold water on the party, but I have to be home by midnight."

"Midnight?" Pam whined. "Oh, Susan. Are you kidding? I don't have to be in until twelve-thirty." Pam pushed out her bottom lip. "Go call your mom and ask her if you can stay until twelve-thirty. All of the rest of us can."

Susan panned the faces of her three friends. She knew that they all felt she should make the plea. Shifting nervously in the booth, she wished that they all would quit staring at her. She shrugged. "You know how mothers are," she said, trying to sound as hurt and as disappointed as possible.

Her speech seemed to work on Roger and Jerry, but it didn't dissolve the abused puppy look in Pam's brown eyes. Susan stared at her and wanted to say, "Be real, Pam. It's only thirty minutes before you have to be home."

Jerry picked up a menu in the center of the

table. "Well, if you can't stay later, you can't stay later."

Susan eased back against the back of the booth, glad that Jerry, her date, had stood up for her.

"Maybe next time you can stay out as long as the rest of us," Jerry said.

Susan took a menu from the table and held it in front of her face. Once she made her decision, she placed the menu back on the table and glanced around the Brigade at the crowd. It's a nice place for a first date, she thought. Nice atmosphere, rustic candles on the tables, good music and old friends. She stared across the table at Roger and Pam, noting the way they looked at each other and the way Pam seemed to laugh every time Roger opened his mouth. She smiled and remembered the four of them on the beach at Anastasia Island last summer. It was only a few weeks ago, and yet it seemed almost as though it had never happened.

A waiter appeared and sat four glasses of water on the red and white checkered tablecloth that covered the wood table. "You all ready to order?"

"I'm going to have a cheeseburger and fries," Pam said before anyone else had a chance to speak. "With a Coke. Large Coke. With lots of ice."

Roger smiled and shook his head. "I'll have the same."

"Make that three," Jerry said.

"I just want a plain hamburger, please. Mustard and pickle only," Susan said.

"What to drink?" the waiter asked.

"Root beer. I'll have a root beer in one of those frosted mugs."

The waiter snapped shut his order book and left.

"Always got to be one in every crowd who's different," Pam said, fluffing her freshly permed brown locks with her fingertips.

"Always," Roger said.

Susan gave Pam one of her go-jump-in-the-ocean smiles that they'd given each other for years and said nothing.

Pam took a deep breath and let it out slowly. "Okay," she sighed. "Moving right along." She threaded her arm through Roger's and kissed him on the cheek. "So, tell me, where have you been hiding?"

"I've been hanging around you for a long time," Roger said, unthreading his arm from Pam's. He laughed. "Probably too long."

"Not long enough," Pam said, raising her eyebrows.

Susan watched the two of them and noticed that Jerry was sitting beside her, quietly, almost as though he didn't know her. She took the mug of root beer that the waiter had just placed in front of her. She waited for him to place the glasses in front of the others, then lifted the mug into the air.

"I'm going to propose a toast," she said. "To us, and to a terrific year."

"Hear! Hear!" Roger said.

Jerry smiled and took a sip of his Coke, and so did Pam.

"We're off to a great year," Pam said. "The three of us are in classes together, and next week we begin driver's ed." She winked at Roger. "It's going to be superb."

"I think you'll really like driver's ed," Susan said. She remembered the night before when she and Neil and Mrs. Johnson got to drive the car. "It's kind of fun, but a little scary when you first get behind the wheel and know that the car is really under your control."

Pam stared at her.

What's wrong? Susan wondered. Did I . . . "You knew I was in that evening driver's ed class? Didn't I tell you about that?"

"Yes. I think you did," Pam said. "I didn't know all of you 'adults' were driving already, though."

Susan smiled and tried to pretend that she didn't notice the chill that had fallen between them. "I guess our teacher doesn't want to waste any time. The class is only two nights a week for four weeks."

"Why did you say you weren't going to take driver's ed with us?" Pam said, pulling off a corner of her paper napkin, then rolling it into a tiny ball.

"I have to take some tests before school next week," Susan explained.

Roger took a sip of Coke. "Oh, yeah. I heard about those. You're in that goody-good class, aren't you?"

Susan frowned. "What?"

"I'm in sixth-hour gym, and all the guys that are in that class are in my sixth-hour gym class. They were telling me about those tests and how they are called gifted or something." He turned to Pam. "You know. There was a deal in the bulletin about how that gifted class was going to be honored at the Honor Society meeting this afternoon. Remember?"

"Yeah. I think so."

Jerry looked at Susan with a wide-eyed stare. "What is gifted?" he asked, running his fingers through his hair.

Susan said stiffly, "It's just the name they've put on the class I'm in." She shrugged her shoulders, hoping to make light of the distinction. "You know. It's like the different reading groups when we were in elementary. I was in the green group. This is just a different name for a whole room full of greens," she said, smiling.

"I guess we're in a room full of blues," Jerry said. "Gee. I don't know what to think about that, Susan. How'd you get in that class?"

"Being a brain, dummy," Pam said. "You won't ever be in it, so why should you care?"

Susan tried to ignore Pam's cutting remark. "They told us we were placed in there because of high test scores we've made on aptitude tests. That's why we have to take those tests next week. They want to be sure each one of us is supposed to be in there. Be sure they haven't goofed." Susan took a sip of root beer. "Heck. I'll probably blow it on one of those tests and they'll throw me out of there."

"Not a chance," Pam said. "Not a chance."

The table was silent for a few moments, and Susan was thankful for the commotion the waiter stirred as he placed the burger platters in front of them. She glanced unobtrusively at her watch and hoped that Roger's dad wouldn't be late. "Did you call your dad and tell him that I had to be home at midnight and to pick us up early?" she asked.

"Did you see him call?" Pam laughed, resting her head on Roger's arm.

"No. That's why I asked. Duh. Pam." Susan forced a smile. "But he could have called a while ago when he went to play the jukebox."

"I didn't," Roger said somberly. "I'll go call now. Wouldn't want our little Susie to be late."

"Me, either," Susan said firmly.

As Roger left the table, she glanced at her watch again and wondered if Neil had called. Would they go to St. Augustine or not? And, if they went, would her ankle feel up to walking all over the small city? She bent and turned her foot, feeling it out as she sat there. If Neil can go, I'll go, she vowed. Even if it kills me.

Susan looked at Jerry and he smiled at her. She smiled back and tried to ignore the guilty feeling she had. How can I sit here with him and be thinking about being with another boy tomorrow?

"It's been a nice evening," she said to Jerry as Roger took his seat beside Pam.

"Yeah. Everybody better say their good-byes now," Roger said. "Dad is on his way." Roger smiled at Pam. "This is it, Pirate. One good night kiss and then it's the gangplank for you." Roger took Pam by the shoulders and pulled her close to him, kissing her firmly on the lips.

"That's another reason I'll be glad when we all learn to drive." Pam giggled. "Our good night kisses can be inside the *car* instead of inside the burger place."

Roger pulled her closer to him and kissed her again. "I can't wait."

Susan's heart felt as though it were skipping across her chest. Her cheeks were growing warm, and she knew that Pam would be the one to guide the next few seconds.

"Well," Pam said, staring at Jerry. "If you are going to kiss her good night, you better get on with it. Unfortunately, we don't have all night."

Susan stiffened as Jerry looked at her. But I've never kissed a boy before, she thought, as Jerry's lips gently brushed hers.

Susan's body tingled from the top of her head to the tip of her toes. Her cheeks felt like hot neon signs pulsing against a cool night wind. And her palms were as damp and clammy as sea moss washed up on a sandy shore.

So that's how kisses make you feel, she thought, smiling at Jerry. She glanced at Pam and Roger, who were kissing again, and wondered if Pam had the same feeling she

had had. Do you have the same feeling every
time you're kissed? Or is the feeling different
each time? Is it different with different people? Susan leaned back against the booth.
She couldn't help wondering. Would the feeling be different if she were kissing Neil?

8

When Susan awoke, she threw back the cotton sheet and eagerly climbed out of bed. "This is the day," she said to herself. "I could have killed you at the time, Gina, but I love you now."

Susan walked around the room, testing her ankle. It'll be okay, she thought. She lifted her weight to her toes and back down again, causing a sharp pain to shoot up the outside of her leg. It'll be okay if I don't spend the day doing dumb things like that.

She shut off her alarm clock before it had time to sound at eight o'clock and began to think about the things she could do in the extra half-hour that was now hers.

After leisurely showering and drying her long blond hair, she strolled into the kitchen with the hot curlers still torturing her head.

"You look bright-eyed this morning," Patty Harris said, glancing up from the morning paper. "Did you have a good time last night?"

"I had an okay time," Susan said. "But I'm planning to have a great time today. Are you sure he said he'd be here at ten?"

"Ten o'clock. That's what he said. What is it again that you two plan?"

"It's an Honor Society project," Susan said, dropping a piece of bread into the toaster. "Aren't you thrilled that I'm in the Honor Society?" she asked.

"You betcha," Patty said with a wink. "So why isn't the whole Honor Society going today? Why is it just going to be you and Neil Kellogg? Hmmmmm?"

"Because this project is Neil's idea, and I got appointed to help him because I've lived in the Matanzas Bay area all of my life. Hmmmmmm?" She caught the toast as soon as it popped up. "I know he doesn't know exactly what kind of project he has in mind. That means going all over St. Augustine until something clicks."

"You're going to need more than one day, then."

"Maybe. But I think we can get a good feel for where we want to go today. Plan on me being home kinda late, though. Probably around six."

"At least six," her mother said. "I won't send out the national guard for you until seven. How's that?"

"A wise woman," Susan laughed. She bit into the toast. "See what you think of this. We can take one of the horse-drawn carriages around the city first. They give you a pretty good tour of the old restored part. Then we can get on one of the sight-seeing trains and whiz by the rest of the town." She munched the toast again and took a quick drink of the juice. "I'm thinking save my feet for as long as I can. After the sight-seeing train, we can walk down St. George Street. Surely by then something will have clicked."

"Since this is an Honor Society project, they might be interested in some of the restored homes in the area," Mrs. Harris said. "The Ribera House is there on St. George Street." She smiled and said, "And if your feet haven't given out by that time, you might walk to Aviles Street. You could take in the Ximenez-Fatio House and the Solana House." She paused for a moment, and added, "Of course, the oldest house is just a hop, skip and a jump from there."

"Please, Mom," Susan said, holding her hand in the air. "I get the picture. Besides, I don't think I'm going to be doing much hopping, skipping or jumping today." She rubbed her ankle. "I nearly fell out of the bleachers last night . . ."

"Susan! What happened!"

Susan shrugged her shoulders. She didn't want her mother getting any ideas about cancelling her excursion with Neil. "I just stepped wrong when I was walking out of the game last night. Turned my ankle a little. It's much better today."

"I hope so. I'll give you a bandage for it anyway."

"Mother."

"I'll give you a bandage, Susan," Patty Harris repeated.

Susan sighed. "Give me the bandage."

When Susan and Neil stepped out of his father's car onto Avenida Menendez, the full effects of the sights and sounds of St. Augustine swept over her.

"I love this place," she said, walking across the narrow sidewalk toward the horse-drawn carriages. The breeze off Matanzas Bay whipped lightly through her long golden hair and teased her nose with the combined odor of ocean and fish. "I've lived here all of my life, and I still love to come to St. Augustine and spend the day just kicking around."

"It's really an interesting place," Neil said. "I hope to spend many days here." He smiled at her and nodded toward Anastasia Island across the Bay. "And over there on the beach."

Susan led the way to the red horse-drawn carriages lined along the curb on Avenida Menendez. "Have you decided what kind of project you want to do yet?" she asked.

"No, not yet, have you?"

They stood behind two families for their turn at a carriage. "I thought we'd go on the carriage tour first," she said. "It will take us through most of this old section. For the sights on the fringes of town, we can take one of the sight-seeing trains that just drove by," she said, pointing to a three-car motor vehicle.

"Fine by me," Neil said. "You're the one who knows what's here. I'm just the one with the idea to work all or some of this into a group project."

The tour guide took Susan's hand and helped her as she stepped on the high step and lifted herself into the carriage. Neil climbed in beside her, and when the tour guide took his place on the narrow front seat, he snapped the reins, and they were on their way.

The slow steady clip-clop of the horse's hooves on Avenida Menendez was a sharp contrast to the cars that filled the main street along the bay. The jerky movement of the carriage rocked Susan and Neil, sometimes causing their shoulders to touch. They leaned back on the seats of the covered carriage and listened as the guide started his spiel.

"St. Augustine is the oldest city in the United States. It was founded in 1565 by the Spanish admiral, Don Pedro Menendez de Aviles, and was claimed for Spain. Don Pedro Menendez named the territory St. Augustine because he first spotted the land from his ship on St. Augustine's day. August 28."

Susan glanced at Neil out of the corner of her eye and smiled to herself at the eager expression on his face.

"So, you see," the guide continued, "St. Augustine was a permanent colony here forty-two years before Jamestown was colonized, and fifty-five years before the Pilgrims landed on Plymouth Rock."

The carriage traveled north, then turned west on Orange Street, with the guide pointing out the Oldest Wooden Schoolhouse and the restored St. George Street, as well as the Old Drugstore at Orange and Cordova.

Susan turned to Neil. "Gina told me you haven't lived next door to her very long. Are you from a state near Florida?"

Neil grinned and shook his head. "No. My parents and I moved here from Oklahoma. Tahlequah, Oklahoma. It's in the northeastern corner of the state."

Susan stared at his lips as though that would make the word easier to understand. "Where did you say?"

"Tahlequah." Neil started to laugh. "Tahl-e-quah." He glanced away from her as the guide pointed out the love tree to them—a palm growing out of the center of an oak tree. "I'm going to move back to Oklahoma one of these days."

"I thought you liked it here," Susan said.

"I do. It's great. It's just that after I get out of college, I want to go back home." He looked at Susan and said, "I'm going to be a veterinarian. A large animal vet. There're lots of farm animals in that part of the country that will be able to use the services of Dr. Neil Kellogg." He started to grin. "I'll have cows from miles around requesting my services."

"A veterinarian?"

"You're looking at me as though you think

I've lost my mind," Neil said. "I really do love it here, but you can see why I am planning to return to Oklahoma, can't you?"

Susan nodded. "Of course, of course. It's not that. It's just that I've never met anyone else who wanted to be a vet. That's what I've always wanted to be. Only I want to be a small animal vet. You know. The kind that everybody knows about." She smiled at him again. "I'm not sure I knew there was a difference between large animal vets and small animal vets, but I guess there is, isn't there?"

"Sure. It's no different in people doctors specializing in different fields."

"That's interesting," Susan said, getting comfortable in the carriage seat again. She tried to keep from noticeably staring at Neil as the carriage lazily traveled through the tree-lined streets.

Above the steady clip-clopping of the horse's hooves on the street, the guide pointed out the Venetian Renaissance architecture of the church along with many other notable items.

"Coming up here on the left is Flagler College. It was originally the Ponce de Leon Hotel, built by Henry Flagler."

Susan grabbed Neil's arm. "I think this is my favorite building in St. Augustine." She drew in her breath. "Look at it. Just look. Isn't it something." Susan leaned to the side of the carriage and pulled Neil with her. "Flagler started building this in 1885 and it wasn't completed until 1888. It cost three million dollars to build. Can you believe it? Three million. Wouldn't you love to have been able to see it when it was new?"

Neil looked at her and grinned.

"They say that there are two and a half miles of hallway in that building." She shook her head as though she didn't believe it herself. "And they say when it opened it cost one hundred dollars a night to stay there." She raised her eyebrows. "I heard that during the depression you could stay there for two or three dollars a night."

The guide slowed the pace of the horse and turned to look at Susan. "Tell me, young lady, how long have you lived around here, anyway?"

Susan smiled broadly. "All of my life."

The guide chuckled to himself. "You've certainly made this trip easy for me. I'd planned to point out the sights of our city to you two young people, and you have pretty much taken care of all of that for me."

Susan's face pinked with embarrassment.

Neil watched Susan for a moment before

speaking. "You know, I think I've got something now."

"You do? Something to do with the old hotel or what?"

"No. I was listening to what you two were saying. And I was trying to think of what Mr. Fleming said, about the Honor Society projects fitting in as extra credit assignments in history. Seems to me that the project should involve people, or should be a service to people. Don't you?"

"I suppose," Susan said.

They were silent for a few more moments, with only the tour guide's words interrupting their thoughts.

"Over here is the second hotel Henry Flagler built. It was called the Alcazar Hotel and was built in 1888. It's now the Lightner Museum."

Finally, Susan stared at Neil. "I know you're on to something. What are you thinking?"

"I'm thinking that there are only about thirty or forty kids in the Honor Society. And there is no telling how many historical places in this city to see or display or describe. Right?"

"Right."

"So, as a project, why don't we ask Mr.

Fleming if each of us could contact the owner or operator of the historical place that we like most? We could see if that person or persons would let us work with them, either after school or on a Saturday, for maybe only a week." Neil's eyes grew wider as he spoke. "And during that time, we would be learning more about the particular site we would have chosen, as well as meeting people and helping the owners or operators. Our time would be free, of course. What do you think?"

Susan's heart quickened. "I think it's a great idea." She glanced around her and then back at Neil. "Each of us would contact a different site so that all of us wouldn't converge on the same one or two people. And once our 'working' project was completed, we could do a written report on what we learned and include the history of the site."

"Exactly. Listen," Neil said enthusiastically, "I think we're really on to something here."

As the guide slowed the carriage to a stop in its place on Avenida Menendez, he pointed out the old fort, Castillo de San Marcos, just ahead of them.

"I'd really like to go through that fort again," Neil said. "It was one of my favorite places when my parents and I were here on vacation." He jumped out of the coach. "If we go ahead with this project, I might want to contact the people at the fort."

"We can go through the fort again now if you want," Susan said, moving to the side of the coach to get out.

Neil reached up and took her hand to help her down. "We could." He glanced up at her. "How much time have you got today?"

Susan brushed her long blond hair away from her face with her fingertips and smiled up into Neil's eyes. "I don't have to be home until six. I've got all the time in the world."

9

Susan walked out of the testing room on Monday morning with a spring in her step. That one wasn't so bad, she thought. One down and five more to go. She waited outside the room for a few minutes, thinking that Gina might be close to finishing as well. When Gina didn't come out, Susan walked on to her locker.

She retrieved the geometry book she'd placed in her locker before the seven o'clock test, then slammed the locker door, still angry with herself for not understanding the assignment well enough to complete it.

"Hey, I was hoping I'd find you this morning," a voice said from behind her.

Susan turned to find herself face to face with Jerry.

"That was some game the other night, wasn't it?"

Susan knew she was looking at him strangely, but she couldn't help it. For some reason, Jerry was the last person she had expected to see this morning. "It was a good game," she said, remembering her date with him as more or less a disaster. Staring into Jerry's pale blue eyes, she could see that he obviously didn't think it was a disaster at all.

"I really had a nice time," Susan said. She started to walk to class, and Jerry followed close behind her. "Thanks again for asking me."

"Heck. I'm just glad you could go. How's your ankle?"

"My ankle?" Susan glanced down as though looking at it would tell her how it was. "It's better today. Much better. Thanks for asking."

Jerry walked beside her and nodded now and then to guys he knew as he met them in the hallway. "Guess Pam told you the big news."

"What news?" Susan remembered that she hadn't seen or spoken to Pam since Friday night, and Pam was acting a little strange then.

"Pam and Roger are going together."

Susan slowed her pace.

"Roger told me yesterday when we went to the arcade. Guess he asked her Friday night, or maybe Saturday. He didn't say."

"I guess so," Susan said. She tossed several long curly locks over her shoulder. "I didn't know anything about it."

"Me either until Roger told me." Jerry smiled at her. "I think they had a pretty good idea, though. What do you think?"

Susan's muscles tensed. "I'm sure that Pam is very excited," she said. Her stomach felt as though it were tying itself into knots, and she wished she could end her conversation with Jerry before he asked her to go with him.

Suddenly Susan saw Gina approaching. "Gina! Wait a second," Susan shouted. "I've got to talk to you." She turned to Jerry and said, "I've really got to see this girl for a few minutes." Hoping that Jerry would take the hint and leave, she said, "Can I talk to you later?"

"Sure." Jerry nodded and then shrugged his shoulders. "Sure. I'll just talk to you later."

Gina walked over to Susan. "What did you need?"

"Need? Oh, nothing, really. I just thought

we might have a few minutes to talk before history started."

Gina looked at her strangely. "I think you were out in the sun too long Saturday. Your mind's getting weird."

"I wasn't. And as for my mind, it better hang in there until after these tests are completed."

"That's for sure." Gina started toward her locker. "So how was your Saturday with Neil? Did you get a lot of work done, or did you just goof around?"

"We did get a lot done." Susan found herself staring off into space. "He is really an interesting guy. Really!"

"Really? So what did you get done?" Gina asked, gathering her books from her locker.

"Oh, several things."

"Did you decide on a project to present at the dinner meeting in two weeks?"

"Yes. We did."

"Great. That's all I wanted to know. I'll leave your private thoughts on the day to you." Gina slammed the door and headed toward their history class.

"You make it sound as though there's some big romance going on here," Susan accused.

"Well, if there isn't, it's because Neil is too preoccupied or too obtuse to see it."

"Gifted students are never obtuse," Susan said. She looked at Gina and giggled. "Duh, never."

Susan walked out of the cafeteria serving line, spotting an empty table in the center of the large room. She sat down and opened her carton of milk as a voice behind her said, "Move over. There's another coming through."

Pam placed her tray next to Susan's. "Mind if I join you?" She slid her tray across the table. "Or did you have your heart set on sitting here all by yourself?"

"Sit down," Susan said. "I've been wanting to talk to you. I heard the good news."

"What good news?"

Susan frowned. "Jerry told me this morning that you and Roger were going together. Isn't that good news?"

"Yeah. Isn't it great?" Pam said. She dove into her plate of spaghetti almost as though she didn't want to talk about the event.

"Since it's so great," Susan said thoughtfully, "why didn't you call me and tell me? I thought we were best friends. Best friends tell each other everything. I had to find out from Jerry."

Susan watched Pam's expression. Pam already had eaten almost all of the spaghetti and was washing it down with a sip of milk.

"Well, Susan," Pam said. "See, I was going to call you and tell you all about it, but I couldn't because my parents thought you already knew."

"How could I have known?"

"I told them I went to your house on Saturday afternoon. I'm sure they think I told you then."

Susan thought about her Saturday afternoon. It had been heavenly, and it certainly hadn't included Pam.

"I wasn't even home on Saturday," Susan said. "Where did you go if you didn't go to my house?"

Pam grinned broadly. "I met Roger at the park. We sat on one of the benches, just the two of us, you know?" Her eyebrows disappeared into the clump of brown curls resting on her forehead. "We were all alone for a couple of hours. I tell you, Susan. It was so great."

"It sounds great," Susan said hesitantly. "But didn't you worry about getting caught? What if I'd called you while you were supposed to be at my house? What if your parents would have called my house looking for you? You could have been in big trouble, Pam."

"I could have been," Pam said. "But as it turned out, I wasn't. Everything went okay, and Roger and I had a couple of hours to really get to know one another."

Susan ate her bowl of green beans one by one. I don't really like her using me that way, she thought. I really don't.

"Want to hear some more good news?" Pam asked.

"Of course," Susan said, uncertain as to whether she did or not.

"I think Jerry is going to ask you to go with him."

Susan thought she felt the green bean she'd just swallowed lodge sideways in her throat.

"Wouldn't that be perfect if he did?" Pam said excitedly. "Then we'd really be a foursome. We'd be able to go everywhere together."

"That would be nice, all right." Susan forced a smile.

"Listen," Pam said. "Tommy is going to take Roger and me out for a while on Thursday night. You want to get Jerry and the two of you come along? We'd probably be home around seven or eight."

"Sure. No, wait," Susan said. "I can't go on Thursday. I have driver's ed that night."

"Oh, yeah," Pam said. "I remember. Because of those special tests," she sighed.

"The goody-goody class has to do everything differently."

"That's not fair, Pam. And I don't like the way you call me goody-goody. I'm Susan. Remember? I'm just plain Susan." She glared at Pam. "And as far as I am concerned, you are just plain Pam. Although I'm having a hard time convincing myself. You've been acting strange ever since we went to the game Friday night."

"I'm not acting strange," Pam said. "And I didn't mean anything by calling you a goody-goody. I certainly didn't intend to hurt your feelings or anything. You know how I am. I just say stuff without thinking. I really thought you knew that that's what everybody in school calls your group."

"I don't have a group, and don't use that old 'I just say stuff without thinking' line on me again. I'm Susan, remember? The person who knows you like a book."

Pam straightened in her chair and looked as though she were preparing for an attack.

"You may not think of your class as a group, but the rest of the school sees you that way. You might as well know it." Pam folded her hands on the table in front of her. "Think about it, Susan. Your classes are different from the rest of the school's, you're all taking egghead tests for the next two weeks—

nobody else is—and every one of you has sixth-hour gym. Only you goody-goodies could swing sixth-hour gym for the whole group."

"You're wrong," Susan said angrily. "And I'd like it a lot if we could just continue calling each other by our correct names. In a civilized tone. I don't think I'd ever grow fond of goody-goody."

Pam looked shocked for an instant, then said, "Oh, Susan, don't be silly. You know I wouldn't ever call you that." Pam raised her eyebrows and grinned. "Not in public, any-way. You know I was only teasing." She scooted her chair away from the table and picked up her tray before Susan could say anything. "I've got to run." Pam paused, then placed her tray on the table again. "Say, you know Thursday night? When Tommy is going to take Roger and me out?"

"Yes. What about it?"

"Well, I'm going to tell my folks that I'm going to your house again, so don't answer the phone that night."

"Pam. I can't do that. Besides. What if my mother answers it?"

Pam shifted her weight from one foot to the other and stared out across the crowded cafeteria. "Okay. Here. I've got it now." She eased into the chair beside Susan. "Go ahead and answer the phone. You answer it. Not your mom. If my mother calls, tell her I just left and am on my way home. That will do it."

"I don't like it," Susan said. "I don't like lying for you."

"And I thought you were my best friend."

"I am your best friend, Pam. But that doesn't mean I have to lie for you."

"Gosh, Susan. I don't know what's gotten into you." Pam shook her head. "I don't get it. Are you jealous? Are you really jealous that I've got Roger and you don't have Jerry yet? He's going to ask you, Susan. I know he is. You'll be in my position soon."

Susan's heart pounded so loudly she thought she could hear it above the noise in the room. "It's okay, Pam," Susan said. "Go on, and don't get caught. I'll try to answer the phone if it rings."

"Gee, thanks," Pam said, rising to her feet once again. She lifted the tray into the air. "Oh, and hold Friday night open. I think the guys are going to take us to the football game again."

Susan watched Pam walk away from the table. *Don't get caught,* she thought. *Please, don't get caught.*

10

The two weeks that followed were a blur of tests, driver's ed classes and homework, some of which wasn't done. The unfinished geometry assignments haunted Susan like a recurring nightmare. Each time she thought she had the concepts learned, there would be more and harder concepts to learn that would hamper her progress.

She shook her head and walked to her closet to find just the right thing to wear to the Honor Society dinner. "If I get a bad progress report in that class, it's going to be sad." She thumbed through the dresses and blouses on the rack. "What am I saying? It's going to be worse than sad! Much worse!"

Susan pulled an oxford cloth shirt and plaid skirt from her closet and placed a blazer beside the combination. She thought about the evening ahead and how she was looking forward to Neil's presentation of his project idea. *Who would have ever thought that I'd be excited about the Honor Society or any of its functions?*

When Susan and her mother pulled up in front of Gina's house, Gina walked out the door before Susan had a chance to get out of the car and go get her.

"Oh, no," Susan said.

Patty Harris looked at Gina and then at Susan. "Did you all plan this?"

Susan's mouth gaped as she watched Gina hurry toward them. If it were not for the girl's red hair and gold-rimmed glasses, she probably could have passed for Susan's twin.

"I didn't know she was going to wear a pleated skirt and blazer, too," Susan said.

"Hi, there," Gina said. "Oh!"

"'Oh' is right," Susan said. "Why didn't you tell me you were going to wear that?"

"Why didn't you tell me you were going to wear that?" Gina held out the tail of the blazer. "This was the most Honor Society-looking thing I owned."

"Me, too," Susan said. "I guess you know

that we look like a couple of little kids who called each other to find out what the other was wearing so they could dress alike." She hesitated for a moment, then sighed. "What are we going to do?"

"You're going to go on to the dinner and not think anything more about it," Patty Harris said before Gina could answer. "You two girls aren't the only girls in the school who own plaid pleated skirts and blazers. There probably will be several girls there dressed just like you. You all just have good taste and know the proper attire for the occasion. That's all. Don't fret about it."

Susan and Gina stepped onto the walk leading to Reeser's Cafeteria's front door.

"My mom will pick up," Gina said. "Thanks for the ride, Mrs. Harris."

"Maybe if we don't stand too close to each other nobody will notice that we're dressed alike," Susan said as they entered the building.

"Maybe not. But then maybe your mom will be right. Maybe there will be other girls here who are dressed like us, and it won't matter." They walked towards the banquet room.

"Well, I'll be—" Gina whispered. She glanced around the room. "Your mom was right after all!"

Susan noticed that nearly all the girls wore pretty much the same outfit as hers and Gina's. "I guess this is the kind of stuff one does wear to one of these," she said reluctantly. "I feel kind of dumb standing around here. Let's go get some punch." She was hoping that somewhere along the way they would spot Neil and that they would be able to sit with him during dinner.

There was no Neil at the punch bowl. Susan and Gina each poured themselves a glass and grabbed a few cookies. They wandered towards a vacant corner and stood there somewhat uncomfortably watching the crowd.

Susan finished hers first and held the empty glass in her hand for a few minutes.

"You know, this is not what we are here for," she said.

"I know. We're here to eat."

"That's not what I mean. I mean, this time has obviously been set aside for mingling, and that's what we're supposed to be doing."

"I'm not good at mingling."

"I'm not, either. But we're going to have to, or everybody here will think we're some kind of nerds for huddling in a corner like this."

"If Neil were here, we could talk to him," Gina said.

"Neil's not here. I've looked."

Gina took a deep breath. "The only person I see that I recognize well enough to talk to is Steve, over there by the punch bowl. Remember him from junior high?"

"I remember. I didn't know him very well," Susan said. "But that shouldn't stop you. At least it never has yet. Go over and fill up your cup and strike up a conversation with him."

"I think we should have waited a while to get here," Gina said. "You know. We should develop an ability to arrive tastefully late."

"We'll work on that next time," Susan said. "Go on."

"And what are you going to do? Huddle in this corner by yourself?"

"No, I'll wander around and do something. I just don't know what yet."

The room was alive with people. Susan wandered toward the door and suddenly saw Neil and another girl talking just inside the door. She stopped, unable to turn away or go forward. Then, resolutely, she turned away. She began to wander around the room, not really seeing faces or hearing voices. She felt a tap on her shoulder and mechanically she turned to see who was there.

"How ya doin'?" Gina asked. Her green

eyes were shining. "What's the problem? Aren't you having fun? I've been doing what you said, and I've been having a great time." Gina looked beyond Susan and waved to a tall, slim boy. "Just a minute, Steve."

"There isn't anything wrong, really," Susan said. "I just wish we would get on with dinner and this meeting. I'm having a boring time."

"I saw Neil here a few minutes ago. Why don't you go talk to him?"

"He's talking to his girlfriend."

"Girlfriend?" Gina asked, looking around. "Oh, her." She shook her head after locating Neil and the girl. "She's not his girlfriend, dummy. That's Cindy Simmons. She's a junior who lives down the street from me and Neil. Don't you remember? She was one grade ahead of us in junior high. Her dad is Doctor Zac Simmons. You've heard of him. He owns Castleview Veterinary Hospital."

"Oh, yeah," Susan said. "I remember her now." A feeling of excitement danced through her. "Well, maybe I will go talk to him, then. In a little while."

"Say," Gina said, looking at Susan suspiciously. "You're really crazy about him, aren't you?"

"Me? Gosh, no. Of course not."

"No. Wait a minute. You *really* are. Gee, Susan. Why didn't you tell me?"

"Because I don't think I really knew it myself until now. It doesn't matter, anyway. I'm sure he doesn't think a thing about me."

"Well, if he did, you'd probably never know it until he came right out and told you. I guess I know him as well as anybody around here, and he seems to keep almost everything to himself." Gina shrugged her shoulders. "He's just that way."

"Maybe so," Susan said.

I guess that way is better than telling the whole school about it, she thought. Maybe it's better than having Gina tell me that he likes me like Pam does for Jerry.

Gina moved nervously, standing on her tiptoes and glancing about the room.

"Gina. You are acting more nervous about this dinner meeting and Neil's presentation than I am sure Neil is," Susan said.

"Oh, I'm not nervous." Gina moved closer to Susan and lowered her voice. "You know I told you that I've never had much interest in boys?"

"Yeah. So?"

"So. I think I'm getting interested." Gina wrinkled her nose and giggled.

"When you set yourself on a new game

plan, you follow through, don't you?" Susan saw Steve glancing in their direction. "I think he's waiting for you to come back and talk some more."

Gina fluffed her shining red hair and rolled her eyes. "Byeeeeee."

The evening went a little faster for Susan once they were seated for dinner. Try as she might, she didn't get to sit next to Neil. She consoled herself with the fact that Gina didn't get to sit next to Steve, either.

Neil's project idea was accepted and enthusiastically supported by Mr. Fleming, Bob Baker, the president, and all of the members in attendance.

I knew it would be a good night for him, Susan thought, as she pushed her chair away from the dinner table. Neil's idea was as good as we thought it would be.

Susan glanced around the room to find Gina. We might as well leave, she thought, as she watched the group move into clusters and start talking again as they had before dinner. Susan spotted Gina talking to Steve again and wondered how she was going to convince Gina that it was time to go home.

Susan stood away from Gina and stared at her. She didn't take her eyes off her, and finally she caught Gina's eye. She gave her a stern look, and reluctantly Gina moved away from Steve to join her.

"What do you want?"

"Aren't you about ready to get out of here?" Susan asked.

"Ah, well, ah, no. Not really." Gina shifted her weight from one foot to the other. "See, I was just going to look you up. Steve's offered to give me a ride home, and I'd really like to take him up on the offer. Do you think if I called Mom and told her I was getting another ride that you could find somebody to take you home?"

The perfect ending to a perfect evening, Susan thought.

"Sure. I can call my mom and have her pick me up," Susan said. "Why don't I just do that and I'll see you in school tomorrow."

"Gee, thanks, Susan. I'll see you in school."

Susan watched Gina almost skip across the tile floor to the tall boy she'd been with all evening.

"Sounds as though you're on foot."

She turned and saw Neil standing in front of her. "Well, yes. I guess I am." She wondered where he'd come from and how long he'd been standing behind her. "It doesn't matter though. I'll just call my mom and have her pick me up."

"I'll give you a ride home if you'd like," Neil said.

Susan's mouth felt as though it were stuffed with cotton. She tried to get a tight rein on her galloping emotions. "That would be nice," Susan said. "If you don't mind. I don't want you to have to go out of your way or anything. Because, I'm sure my mom could come and get me." She knew she was babbling nervously, but she couldn't seem to stop herself.

"That's okay. It won't be a problem at all."

On the way home, Susan and Neil talked about the Honor Society project and discussed the many sites in St. Augustine that would be good possibilities for their particular interests. When Susan stepped out of Neil's father's car, she found herself wishing that it didn't have to end so soon.

"Thanks for the ride, Neil," Susan said.

Neil got out of the car and closed the door behind him. "I'm glad Gina got another ride," he said, placing his hand on her elbow.

His touch was like a lightning flash in the summer sky, and Susan wondered if he could feel her body tingle through her blazer.

"It's hard for me to get a chance to talk to you in school," Neil said, walking her up the driveway to her door. "It seems like I'm always in a hurry to get to our next class, or get something done, or something." He smiled.

"It was fun. I enjoyed it, too," Susan said. She walked slower and wished that she could tell him that she would love to talk to him more—at school, on the phone, anyplace.

They walked to her porch, and Neil continued to hold her arm. "Well, thanks for a nice evening," he said.

The moonlight cast a silvery glow across the yard and trees, and as Neil stood looking at her, he appeared to be painted with the soft silvery light as well.

She smiled at him. "Thank you for a nice evening. And the ride home." She wished she knew what else to say. What to do. What do you do when you discover you're crazy about a guy who probably is just being polite to you?

The dark shadow of Neil's face blocked out the moon as he bent down toward her. His lips gently touched hers. Susan trembled with excitement. "Good night," she whispered as he slowly drew away.

Neil slowly released her hands and turned to walk to his father's car. "See you in school, Monday." he said as he opened the car door.

Susan stayed a moment to watch him turn

on the ignition and drive off. She really didn't want to go into the house at all but knew her mother would worry if she didn't check in. She didn't feel like speaking to anybody—somehow her relationship with Neil seemed too personal, too private. She floated into the house and past her mother, who was standing in the living room.

"How was the dinner?"

"Wonderful." Susan sighed. "I got a ride home with Neil. Gina had other plans at the last minute."

Susan glided past Mrs. Harris, through the hallway and into her bedroom, closing the door behind her. She dropped her purse on the floor and stepped out of her shoes on the way to her bed. Peeling off her blazer, she glanced at herself in the mirror.

"Susan Harris. I think you're in love," she told her glowing image.

11

Susan arrived at school Monday wearing her best pair of jeans and a new burgundy lightweight sweater she'd been eager to wear. She knew when she put it on that morning that she'd be too hot all day long, but this was a special morning. It was her first morning at school to be in love. And she decided when she slipped into her clothes that being too warm all day was a small price to pay to look gorgeous for the guy you love.

I won't tell Gina yet, Susan thought, switching books at her locker. I'll wait a while and see if she notices any difference. Maybe I won't tell her at all. I could wait and see if she tells me.

158

She closed her locker and wondered how she would keep from grinning throughout the day. She walked into homeroom and didn't realize until she saw the empty desks that she was fifteen minutes early for class. She took her seat anyway. *Maybe we can talk if he gets here early, too. I wonder if he's as eager to see me again as I am him,* she thought.

As each minute passed, one or two more students wandered in and took their seats, but Neil wasn't one of them.

Gina hurried in and glanced over her shoulder at the clock. She slipped into her desk and sighed. "I thought I was going to be late."

"You have time to spare," Susan said cheerfully. "How'd things go with Steve the other night?"

Gina grinned. She leaned closer to Susan. "I wish I'd known earlier that guys were so much fun."

Susan tried not to laugh. *I guess I didn't know that guys could be so much fun either,* she thought.

Susan watched the minute hand on the clock tick closer to eight o'clock and felt a faint breeze blowing across the side of her face.

Gina was sitting at her desk fanning herself with a spiral notebook and thumbing through some notes. She glanced up at Susan. "Why are you wearing that sweater? Aren't you hot?"

"No. No special reason," Susan said lightly as Neil raced through the classroom door.

He took his seat across from Susan and glanced at her. "Hi," he said, flashing a quick smile.

As she watched him stack his books inside his desk and pull his history book to the top of the desk, Susan realized he wasn't going to say anything else.

The rest of the day, Susan watched and waited for a sign from Neil that he felt about her as she did him. None came. Nothing had changed. He seemed to be the same boy he had been before the Honor Society dinner and the kiss good night.

How could I have been so stupid, Susan thought as she changed for her driver's ed class. She sat on the side of her bed and slipped on her tennis shoes. Old shoes to match old jeans. Now all I need is an old shirt. She jerked a faded knit top from her closet. There's no point in getting dressed up for driving class. Mrs. Johnson doesn't care what I look like. Neither does Mr. Townes. Slipping the top over her head and the waistband of her jeans, she said, "And neither does Neil Kellogg."

Mr. Townes took each of them out onto the city streets as he had done the several sessions before.

"You're doing very nicely, Susan," Mr. Townes said. "You'll do fine on your test, I'm sure."

Neil's turn was next, and Susan thought he did better than usual. His dad was probably helping him.

When Mrs. Johnson took the wheel, Susan felt a flash of fear. The woman drove into the curb when she turned out into the street, and Mr. Townes had to hit the special brake pedal on his side of the car to prevent her from turning the car in one big circle.

"I'm just so nervous," she said breathlessly. "I can't do this. I just can't do it."

"Now, now. That wasn't that big of a problem," Mr. Townes said. He released his foot from the brake and told her gently to do the same while turning the steering wheel to get the car lined up with the lane of traffic again.

Susan glanced at Neil out of habit more than anything else, and when he smiled back at her, she felt her heart skip. She thought about a saying she'd heard her mother say from time to time. Old habits are hard to break. You're going to have to break this one, she told herself. He doesn't care about you, and you're going to have to stop acting like a starry-eyed kid every time he looks at you. Face it. He likes you for a friend. The same way he likes Gina. There's nothing more.

With the driver's ed classes completed and her Honor Society project on hold in her mind for a while, Susan devoted all the spare time she had to her geometry.

"Some of you people are going to have to spend more time on your studies," Mrs. Staley said at the end of class. "This is midquarter, and several of you are going to receive progress reports." She held the small square slips of paper in her hand. "I'm sorry, because all of you are capable of doing this work."

Susan held her breath and closed one eye, hoping above all hope that Mrs. Staley would not place one of the papers on her desk.

The woman walked up and down each row, and when she got to the aisle that separated Susan's and Neil's row, she gently laid one of the papers face down on the corner of Susan's desk.

Susan's spirits fell. Fear and a desperate desire to cry welled inside her. When the bell rang, she grabbed the paper and darted out of class before Gina or Neil could console her or ask questions.

She almost ran down the hall away from the classroom and away from the cafeteria. She knew Gina would be waiting for her to return to have lunch with her. But at that second, she didn't want to see Gina. How could she face her? Gina wasn't a failure. She was.

Susan slowed her pace and rambled through the halls for a time. When she regained her composure, she opened the progress report and saw that only one line had been checked. "Is capable of doing better work." Capable, maybe, Susan thought. If I only understood it.

She saw Jerry approaching, and for the first time in a long time, she was glad to see him.

"How's it going?"

Susan smiled. "I'd have been disappointed if you hadn't asked me," she said. "Do you know you say those very words to me almost every time we see each other?"

"I think I say that to everybody," Jerry said, looking away for an instant.

Susan watched him and felt as though she'd lost touch with him and Pam and Roger over the past few weeks. "So. How's it going with you?"

"Things are okay, I guess," Jerry said. "I'm fighting homework like crazy." Jerry stopped suddenly and acted as though he had touched on a forbidden subject. "I guess homework's never been a big problem for you. You probably don't even understand what I'm talking about."

"I understand," Susan said, feeling again as though she might cry. "Don't you think I have trouble with homework, too?"

Jerry shrugged his shoulders and didn't answer.

"I'm not any different from you, Jerry."

"Uh, okay," he stammered. "I didn't really stop to talk to you about homework, anyway." He glanced at the floor and then around the hallway. "I just wanted to tell you that Pam and Roger are going to the game on Friday night, and I wanted to know if you wanted to go with me." He paused for a second. "I know Pam has probably told you a bunch of times that I've been going to ask you out again. But you know how Pam's always saying stuff." He glanced away from Susan. "So, what do you say? We don't all get to see much of each other anymore. And there's something I'd like to ask you."

Something you'd like to ask me? Susan thought. She stared at him for an instant and thought about all of the times since school started that Pam had said that Jerry was going to ask her to go with him.

"Did you say Pam and Roger are going?" Susan asked, delaying her answer.

"Sure. It's their idea." Jerry's eyes widened. "And mine, too, of course. I want you to go, too. With me. To the game."

Susan took a deep breath and tried to gather her thoughts about her. "Thanks for asking, Jerry," she said, exhaling slowly. "I'd love to go to the game with you."

"That's great," Jerry said, walking away from her. "I'll call you, or maybe Pam can tell you when we get the arrangements worked out."

"Fine," Susan said. "See you later." She headed for the cafeteria, where she found Gina sitting alone in the far corner of the room.

"I was hoping you'd come," Gina said softly. "We don't have to talk about it if you don't want to." She peered through her gold-rimmed glasses. "Are you okay?"

"I'm okay. Just a little embarrassed,"

Susan's voice cracked. "And a little scared, I guess." She turned away from Gina as a tear slid down her cheek. "My mother is going to kill me." She tried to force a chuckle from her trembling body. "It sure looked funny, didn't it? Susan Harris. Brain. Gifted student. Getting a progress report in geometry."

"Don't be so hard on yourself," Gina said. "Half of our class got progress reports."

"You didn't."

Gina shrugged her shoulders. "My turn is probably coming next hour."

"But biology isn't one of the gifted classes."

"The way I look at it, a class is a class. Gifted or regular. If you don't understand the work, it's all the same," Gina said.

Susan picked at her lunch and tried to think about how she was going to tell her mother and what she was going to do about the geometry class.

"Let's talk about something not so depressing," Gina said. "I'm sick of thinking about dreary old school. Go ahead. You pick a subject."

Susan forced a smile to her lips. "I can't think of anything now that's not depressing. You go first."

Gina frowned and then smiled. "Okay. Steve has asked me to go to the football game with him on Friday night. Can you believe it? My first date!" Gina folded her hands on her tray. "He's called me three times since the Honor Society dinner. And my parents!" she said loudly. "My parents are about to have a stroke. They can't imagine what's come over me all of a sudden. And quite frankly, neither can I. All I know is that I love it."

"I can see you're loving it," Susan said. "He's a pretty cute guy."

"I don't know if he's all that cute or not. But he's tall. You know? Tall guys seem to be cute even if they aren't really. I think it's because they're taller and you can't see their faces as easily."

"Gina! That's a terrible thing to say!" Susan laughed.

"I know." Gina's smile faded. "I just wanted to see you laugh again. See. Things aren't so bad that we can't laugh together." A hopeful look appeared in Gina's eyes as she asked, "How are things with you and Neil?"

"I thought you said things aren't so bad," Susan said. She shrugged her shoulders. "And I suppose they aren't. We're the same as we always have been. He's my friend, and

I suppose I'm his friend. You know what you said. He keeps to himself. I guess you were right about never really knowing where you stand with him."

"I never said you never know where you stand with him. I said he was friendly, but that he was the kind of guy who probably never talked to anybody about his girlfriends until he was ready to talk to them about it."

"Let's just say that he hasn't been doing any talking to me. About anything."

Susan pushed her chair back away from the table. "I think I'll go on to class. I'm really not very hungry today."

"Wait," Gina said, grabbing Susan's tray. "Let's talk. Really talk." A pleading look filled her face. "I hate to see you this way. And I know I can help, if you'll let me."

"What are you going to do? Go home with me so my mother won't yell at me?"

"I can do better than that," she said. Gina leaned closer to Susan. "I went by the office the other day and left my name as a tutor in math. I haven't had any calls yet, but Susan, I can help you. We can get together and study. It will be like having a tutor, but it'll be better. Nobody will know. They'll think I'm just helping you study, and you are just helping me study. We can do this. And besides," she said shyly, "I *really* do need help in biology. I'm not just saying that to make you feel better. It's serious."

"You really will help me?"

"Absolutely. I can teach you the concepts. I bet that's all you're lacking. Mrs. Staley isn't very good at teaching the concepts. If I didn't have my dad to fall back on, I probably wouldn't have gotten them, either."

"I think you're right," Susan said slowly. "I think I could do the work if I just understood the procedures better."

"Of course you could. And you can help me study my biology."

"It isn't hard."

"I know it isn't," Gina said. "But I never seem to study the right things, and the reason I don't study the right things is because they aren't really clear to me."

Susan smiled at Gina and stretched out her hand. "It's a deal," she said confidently. "Let's plan to get together three days a week for two hours each time."

"Monday, Wednesday and Friday afternoons."

"Okay," Susan said. "And when I show my mom this progress report tonight, I'll tell her the problem, and I'll tell her that we are already working on the solution."

"Same here," Gina said. She sighed. "I know this is probably too much to ask for.

But if everything goes well, let's ask if we can go to the license bureau on Saturday and get our driver's permit."

"You're a dreamer," Susan said. "If everything goes well after we have the progress report discussion, I'll ask my mom about Saturday." She raised her eyebrow. "If everything does not go well, my driver's permit may be a long time coming."

12

Patty Harris held the small white paper in her hand and looked at it again. "I still don't understand, Susan. I don't understand how you got in this spot to begin with." She ran her fingers through her hair. "Or why you let yourself get into this situation. Why didn't you say something?"

Susan sat on the arm of the sofa and stared at the floor and didn't say anything for a moment. She took a deep breath and let it out slowly. "I thought I could pull out of it. But I didn't."

Her mother paced the floor in front of her. "I know I'm probably making a big deal out of this. But it is such a surprise to me. You've *never* had a problem in school. You've never had to really study hard for your grades. I just didn't worry when I didn't see you with your nose in a book. You've never had to." She sat in the chair across from Susan. "Maybe it's my fault for not checking up on you and asking you about your studies."

"It's not your fault, Mom. And it's not all my fault. I don't understand the work," Susan said. "But I'm going to. Gina is making *A's* in that class. We had lunch together today and talked it all out. She's going to come over three days a week and help me learn the concepts I don't understand. I'm going to help her with her biology."

"Gina is going to help you study? Susan."

"She is, Mom. She told me she had signed up to be a tutor in math, but nobody has called her yet. She'll be like my tutor, only she won't really be a tutor."

Patty Harris folded the paper and threw it on the coffee table. "You make it sound so easy."

"It is, Mom. I promise it is."

Patty stared at Susan and didn't say anything.

Before Susan could stop it, a tear slid down her face. "How do you think I feel? Here I am in these gifted classes, and I can't do the work. Everybody thinks I'm a dummy. They think I can't do the work." Tears washed across her cheeks as she said, "I'm not a dummy, Mom. But I'm not a genius." Wiping the tears from her eyes before more could fall, Susan said, "I'm just a normal girl. A regular kid. Why doesn't anybody accept that?"

Mrs. Harris walked to Susan's side and placed her hand on Susan's shoulder. "I accept that. I'm sorry, Susan." She rubbed Susan's shoulder and lowered her voice. "Your father always expected so much from himself that I guess that expectation filtered through me to you."

Susan tried to smile through her watery eyes. "I'm going to make it, Mom. I know what I want, and I know I've got to make good grades to get there. I'm going to college. And I'm going to vet school. There's no question in my mind."

"There's none in mine, either. I think you're on your way," Mrs. Harris said. She started to walk out of the room.

Before her mother could leave, Susan said, "Oh, Mom!"

Patty Harris turned to her.

"Are you in a better mood now?"

"I seem to be. Why?" She cast a suspicious glance at Susan and smiled.

"Gina wants to know if we can go to the

license bureau on Saturday and get our driver's permits. Do you think that would be okay?"

Her mother's smile grew wider. "I think that would be fine. If you have your geometry finished."

Susan closed the geometry book and fell back across her bed. "I don't think I'll ever get it," she sighed.

"Nonsense. You're doing much better," Gina said. "This is our second session, and I can already see improvement. Can't you?"

"Oh, I suppose," Susan said. "I guess I just expected you to come over once, and magically, I'd understand everything I've been lost on for weeks."

"Well, hang in there, kid. You are making it. Just keep going over those concepts until they begin to make sense." Gina started to laugh. "Of course. When they start to make sense, you're in real trouble then. There's no hope." She closed her book. "I've got to be heading for home. This is my big night out."

"I remember," Susan said. "Your first date with Steve."

"It's going to be great," Gina said. "I know it is." She stood to leave. "Aren't you going to the game tonight, too?"

"Yes," Susan said. "I'm going with Pam

and Roger and Jerry. Maybe I'll see you there," she said hesitantly.

"Maybe. If I miss you, though, I'll be by tomorrow at two. My mom will take us to the license bureau, and if it's okay, we can call your mom to pick us up when we're finished."

"No problem. That'll be fine."

Susan followed Gina to the door. "Good luck tonight," she called. "Have a great time."

She walked back into her room and stared at the geometry book on her bed. The cover of the book seemed to mock her and tease her because there was something inside it that it knew and Susan didn't. The longer she stared at the book, the more determined she became to conquer its secrets.

"I'm going to get you," she whispered. "I'm going to make it if I have to stay awake all night to do it. You've made a dummy out of me for the last time."

Susan walked down the hallway to the living room, both afraid and determined. She picked up the phone and dialed Jerry's number.

"Jerry. This is Susan."

The boy on the other end of the phone was silent after saying hello.

"Listen. I hate to cancel out on going to

the game tonight. But I've got a lot of homework to do, and I'm just not going to be able to make it." Susan waited for a response, and when none came, she said, "Maybe some other time."

"Yeah, sure, Susan. Maybe."

Susan heard the dial tone in her ear, and her heart beat even faster as she dialed the next number.

"Pam. This is Susan."

"Hi, Susan. Hey, listen, we'll be by at about seven-thirty. See if you can't stay out this time until twelve-thirty. Will ya?"

"Pam," Susan interrupted. "Pam. I'm calling to let you know that I can't go tonight."

"Can't go? Why not?"

"I called Jerry and told him. I can't go because I have a ton of geometry to do, and I've got to stay here and do it." The voice on the other end of the phone was silent. "Pam? Are you there?"

"I'm here. And I don't know what you're going to do tonight, but you could have made up a better lie than homework. Be real, Susan. You never do homework. You've never had to do homework."

"I've never had geometry, either," Susan said.

"I've got to go," Pam said curtly. "I'm really surprised at you, Susan. You had to know that Jerry was going to ask you to go with him tonight."

Susan's hand trembled as she squeezed the phone receiver tighter. "I apologized, Pam. What else was I supposed to do? I said maybe we could get together another time."

"Don't count on it, Susan. You're so caught up in that goody-goody class and that Honor Society stuff that it's obvious that you don't have time to associate with kids on our level anymore."

Susan listened and couldn't make herself speak.

"Have a good time tonight doing your *homework*. I'll see ya."

Susan replaced the phone receiver on its cradle. Her hand still trembled from the effects of Pam's words. I knew she would be upset, Susan thought. But she had no reason to be that angry with me. It's just a football game.

"Don't you think you better be getting ready for the game?" her mother said, as she walked through the back door. "I expected you to be dressed and ready to go by the time I got home from work."

"I'm not going to the game. I called and cancelled."

"Cancelled? Aren't you feeling well?"

"I'm staying home to do my geometry."

Patty Harris placed her handbag on the kitchen table. "Oh, Susan. When we had our talk about your schoolwork, I didn't mean that you were grounded. I know you will get your assignments done. You didn't have to cancel your date with your friends. Go ahead and call them back. Maybe it's not too late to change your plans back to what they were."

"I didn't cancel because of you, Mom," Susan said, pouring herself a glass of milk. "I cancelled because of me. I'm determined to get that stuff. And I'm going to get it— understand it—if I have to stay awake all night doing it."

Patty stared into her daughter's eyes.

"I have to. For me." She took a bite of the sandwich and shook her head. "You know? Before school started, I was scared to death of being different. I was scared that something would change and Pam and I wouldn't be friends anymore." She looked at her mother and tried to make herself smile. "Guess I was right."

"Not really," her mother said. "These classes didn't make you different. You and Pam have been different as day and night all the years you've been friends. These classes have just made your differences more obvious." She walked out of the kitchen.

I don't think the day will ever come when

things are normal again, Susan thought, slowly eating the sandwich. Pam is gone, Gina has a new love in her life and the love in my life is only a friend.

She stared across the kitchen to the squatty fan palm outside the window and thought about her afternoon in St. Augustine with Neil. It had been so wonderful then. She had planned from that day on to be with him, working on their Honor Society projects together.

"Forget it," she said sternly. She drank the last of her milk and placed the glass in the sink. As she filled it with water, she told herself: All of these messes in my life are things to think about tomorrow. For tonight . . . tonight there is the mastering of geometry.

"I still can't believe you missed the game last night to do your geometry," Gina said, following Susan into the license bureau. "You are doing okay. You'll have that stuff down pat in no time."

"I have it down pat today," Susan said. She walked into the bureau and glanced around the room, trying to see a sign that would tell her where she and Gina were supposed to go to take the written test for their driving permit. "I studied until one o'clock this morning. And I tell you what. I know that stuff forward and backward."

There were only a few others taking the written exam, and Susan found herself wondering what poor Mrs. Johnson was doing, wondering if the woman would ever learn to drive.

Once the test was finished, Susan and Gina placed their answer sheets and booklets on the counter and took a seat again to wait for the results.

"I didn't think that was very hard. Did you?" Gina whispered.

"No. It wasn't bad at all. If the driving part is this easy, we'll have it made."

"I'm so excited about this part that I sometimes think I'm going to go crazy before I turn sixteen and can get my real driver's license," Gina said.

"I know what you mean."

Susan glanced around the crowded office, wishing that the results would be tallied soon so they could leave. People entered, bought car tags, renewed drivers' licenses, registered vehicles and left again, one after another.

Suddenly Susan's gaze locked on the boy and the state trooper who entered the license bureau.

"That's Neil," Susan said, poking Gina in the ribs. "And he's with a state trooper. My gosh! He doesn't even have a driver's license yet, and he's been arrested!"

"Susan! Gina! What are you two doing here?" Neil asked.

"We're here waiting for the results of the written exam we just took. Thought we'd take a shot at getting our drivers' permits," Susan said.

"The test was easy, wasn't it?"

"Yes," Susan said cautiously. "Have you taken it?"

Neil nodded and grinned broadly. "I sure have. Passed with flying colors." He took a deep breath and seemed to stand a little taller. "Officer Mabry here has just given me my driver's test." He winked at Susan. "I passed."

Susan smiled. "I'm thrilled for you." She glanced at Gina and gave her a don't-tell-him-what-we-originally-thought look.

Gina raised her eyebrows and nodded. She turned to Neil. "So how did you get to take your driver's test? I thought you had to be sixteen."

"I'm sixteen today. This is my happy birthday present to me," Neil said.

Susan floated on his smile and wished once again that she didn't find his brown eyes irresistible. He's a friend, she told herself. A schoolmate and a friend.

"Harris. Tate," the woman behind the counter called.

Susan and Gina walked over to her and the woman slid a driver's permit to each of them along with their test scores.

"This permit allows you to drive as long as there is a licensed driver in the car with you," the woman said, as though she had said those very words a million times before.

They walked away from the counter, and Gina said, "I wanted to say 'thank you, your licenseship,' but I didn't dare."

"Wise move."

Neil had been at another counter and walked up behind them as they were walking out of the bureau.

"How about a lift home?" he asked. "Dad left me the car. It's ready and waiting to go wherever we want to go."

Susan's heart beat wildly at the thought. She wanted to go so badly. But there would be her mother to call.

"I'd love to go with you," Susan said. "I'll have to call my mother. She is—"

"She is real picky about stuff like this," Gina interrupted. "You know how mothers are." She looked straight into Susan's eyes. "You go call your mom and tell her Neil will be bringing you home. Then I'll call my mom and tell her to come and get me now. We've got to get over to the shopping center and get those jeans for me today before they close."

When Susan returned, Gina put her hand in Susan's back and all but pushed Susan and Neil out the front door of the bureau. "You two go on. My mom will be here in no time. Congratulations, Neil! You, too, Susan!"

Susan smiled all the way through the parking lot to Neil's car. Crazy girl, she thought. She didn't have to do this. She slid across the front seat of Neil's car.

"Do you have any time to spare?" Neil asked. "Or do you have to get right home?"

"I've got some time." She looked at Neil and smiled. "Mom said to take our time and not hurry. I think that meant 'don't drive too fast.'"

"Sounds an awful lot like that, doesn't it?" Neil steered the car out of the parking lot and out onto the highway. "I thought we'd drive over to St. Augustine if you have the time."

"Sure," Susan said, wondering why they would be going to St. Augustine now. "As I told you before, it's one of my favorite places."

Neil parked the car in the parking lot at the Castillo de San Marcos. The fort had just closed for the day, and the parking lot was almost empty.

"I thought we could walk along the bay

front there and talk. That is, if you wanted
to."

"Fine," Susan said softly.

Neil started to get out of the car, and tiny
drops of rain began to tap at the windshield
of the car. "Wouldn't you know it? Another
afternoon rain."

"It probably won't last long," Susan said.
"They rarely do."

The silence in the car surrounded them,
and Susan felt as though every move, every
motion she made called attention to the fact
that they were alone.

Neil cleared his throat and leaned against
the steering wheel. He stared out the windshield at the patches of blue sky that shone
through the clouds.

"Have you started your Honor Society
project yet?" he asked.

Susan chuckled softly to herself. "No."
She shook her head. "I'm just now at a point
where I can think about that project." She
watched the raindrops hit the parking lot,
their steady tapping coming a little slower
now. "It seems as though I haven't had time
this year for anything. You know? There
were those tests at the beginning of school,
then driver's ed all those nights. And all of
the homework." Susan fought the feeling of
embarrassment as she continued to talk.

"Then we all know about the progress report I got in geometry."

"I hated that," Neil said. "I don't think you deserved it."

"Oh, I deserved it, all right. That was the terrible part." Susan straightened in the seat and smiled broadly. "And it was good for me in a way, strangely enough. It made me realize that I can't expect to breeze through everything in my life without applying myself and doing a little extra hard work when I need to." She smiled at Neil and shrugged. "I can do that geometry now. I really do understand it. So. It was good that things happened the way they did."

"Maybe so." Neil rolled down the window and held out his hand. "I think it's stopped sprinkling now. Want to walk along the bay?"

"I'd love it."

Neil came around to Susan's side of the car and opened the door for her, extending his hand to help her out. They walked through the parking lot and across the grass to the paved walkway that extended along the bay.

A fresh ocean breeze blew gently across the bay, mixing its crisp salty scent with the mingled aromas of seafood cooking in the area restaurants.

"This is my favorite time here," Susan

said, running her hand along the railing and staring down into the water. She pointed to a large fishing boat sailing under the draw-bridge at the Bridge of Lions. "Wouldn't you love to be on that boat, going wherever it's going?"

Neil took her hand and, without speaking, escorted her to one of the wooden benches that looked out over the bay.

"Susan, I was thinking." Neil looked out across the water. "I thought maybe if you didn't have something already in mind for that Honor Society project, maybe you'd want to do something with me."

"I'd love to Neil. I think that's a great idea. We could probably do something together at the fort, or maybe even at one of the places on St. George Street."

"Sure. Whatever," Neil said. "Anything would be okay with me. I just think we could work pretty well together. You know?"

"I've always thought that," Susan said softly. "I never knew you felt that way, though."

Neil stared up at the clouds that were breaking up overhead and then glanced back at Susan. "I know. I'm funny, I guess," he said hesitantly. "I've wanted to do things with you, Susan. I've wanted to ask you out and take you to football games, and I've even wanted to bring you back over here to St. Augustine." He took a deep breath, then exhaled. "But that's always been my problem. *I* wanted to take you to those places. I didn't want my dad taking us, or your mom taking us. *I* wanted to take us. I guess what I'm trying to say, Susan, is that I'd like to work on that Honor Society project with you." He took her hand and held it tightly in his. "And I'd like to ask you out. Often. That is, if you think you'd like to go."

He leaned toward her and Susan closed her eyes as his soft lips gently brushed hers.

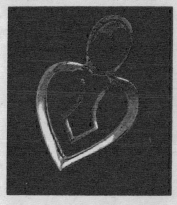

First Love from Silhouette

THERE'S NOTHING QUITE AS SPECIAL AS A FIRST LOVE.

— $1.75 each —

2 □ GIRL IN THE ROUGH Wunsch

3 □ PLEASE LET ME IN Beckman

4 □ SERENADE Marceau

6 □ KATE HERSELF Erskine

7 □ SONGBIRD Enfield

14 □ PROMISED KISS Ladd

15 □ SUMMER ROMANCE Diamond

16 □ SOMEONE TO LOVE Bryan

17 □ GOLDEN GIRL Erskine

18 □ WE BELONG TOGETHER Harper

19 □ TOMORROW'S WISH Ryan

20 □ SAY PLEASE! Francis

— $1.95 —

24 □ DREAM LOVER Treadwell

26 □ A TIME FOR US Ryan

27 □ A SECRET PLACE Francis

29 □ FOR THE LOVE OF LORI Ladd

30 □ A BOY TO DREAM ABOUT Quinn

31 □ THE FIRST ACT London

32 □ DARE TO LOVE Bush

33 □ YOU AND ME Johnson

34 □ THE PERFECT FIGURE March

35 □ PEOPLE LIKE US Haynes

36 □ ONE ON ONE Ketter

37 □ LOVE NOTE Howell

38 □ ALL-AMERICAN GIRL Payton

39 □ BE MY VALENTINE Harper

40 □ MY LUCKY STAR Cassiday

41 □ JUST FRIENDS Francis

42 □ PROMISES TO COME Dellin

43 □ A KNIGHT TO REMEMBER Martin

44 □ SOMEONE LIKE JEREMY VAUGHN Alexander

45 □ A TOUCH OF LOVE Madison

46 □ SEALED WITH A KISS Davis

47 □ THREE WEEKS OF LOVE Aks

48 □ SUMMER ILLUSION Manning

49 □ ONE OF A KIND Brett

50 □ STAY, SWEET LOVE Fisher

51 □ PRAIRIE GIRL Coy

52 □ A SUMMER TO REMEMBER Robertson

First Love from Silhouette

53 ☐ LIGHT OF MY LIFE Harper	60 ☐ ALABAMA MOON Cole	67 ☐ PUPPY LOVE Harrell
54 ☐ PICTURE PERFECT Enfield	61 ☐ HERE COMES KARY! Dunne	68 ☐ CHANGE PARTNERS Wagner
55 ☐ LOVE ON THE RUN Graham	62 ☐ SECRET ADMIRER Enfield	69 ☐ ADVICE AND CONSENT Alexander
56 ☐ ROMANCE IN STORE Arthur	63 ☐ A NEW BEGINNING Ryan	70 ☐ MORE THAN FRIENDS Stuart
57 ☐ SOME DAY MY PRINCE Ladd	64 ☐ MIX AND MATCH Madison	71 ☐ THAT CERTAIN BOY Malek
58 ☐ DOUBLE EXPOSURE Hawkins	65 ☐ THE MYSTERY KISS Harper	72 ☐ LOVE AND HONORS Ryan
59 ☐ A RAINBOW FOR ALISON Johnson	66 ☐ UP TO DATE Sommers	

FIRST LOVE, Department FL/4
1230 Avenue of the Americas
New York, NY 10020

Please send me the books I have checked above. I am enclosing
$_____ (please add 75¢ to cover postage and handling. NYS and
NYC residents please add appropriate sales tax). Send check
or money order—no cash or C.O.D.'s please. Allow six weeks for
delivery.

NAME _____

ADDRESS _____

CITY _____ STATE/ZIP _____

Four exciting First Love from Silhouette romances yours for 15 days—_free!_

If you enjoyed this First Love from Silhouette,® you'll want to read more! These are true-to-life romances about the things that matter most to you now—your friendships, dating, getting along in school, and learning about yourself. The stories could really happen, and the characters are so real they'll seem like friends.

Now you can get 4 First Love from Silhouette romances to look over for 15 days—absolutely free! If you decide not to keep them, simply return them and pay nothing. But if you enjoy them as much as we believe you will, keep them and pay the invoice enclosed with your trial shipment. You'll then become a member of the First Love from Silhouette℠ Book Club and will receive 4 more new First Love from Silhouette romances every month. You'll always be among the first to get them, and you'll never miss a new title. There is no minimum number of books to buy and you can cancel at any time. To receive your 4 books, mail the coupon below today.

First Love from Silhouette® is a service mark and a registered trademark of Simon & Schuster

---

This offer expires July 31, 1984

First Love from Silhouette Book Club, Dept. FL-020
120 Brighton Road, P.O. Box 5020, Clifton, NJ 07015

Please send me 4 First Love from Silhouette romances to keep for 15 days, absolutely _free_. I understand I am not obligated to join the First Love from Silhouette Book Club unless I decide to keep them.

NAME_____
(Please print)

ADDRESS_____

CITY_____ STATE_____ ZIP_____

Signature_____
(If under 18, parent or guardian must sign)

First Love from Silhouette

Coming Next Month

A Passing Game by Beverly Sommers

As kicker and only girl on the Evanston High football team, Tobey basked in glory. And to top it all, she was on a personal kick of her own: should she run for the touchdown, block or intercept an unexpected pass?

Under The Mistletoe by Michelle Mathews

Her father was shocked, her mother astounded when a handsome stranger took Megan in his arms and tenderly kissed her under the mistletoe. But as for Megan—she rather enjoyed it. It was definitely going to be one of the better Christmas vacations.

Send In The Clowns by Marilyn Youngblood

Lita's heart was doing somersaults. She couldn't stop grinning. Her life was a circus! Now that she had met Jerry, she was dancing on a tightrope. But would he hold the net? Did he really plan to include her in his act?

Short Stop For Romance by Elaine Harper

Celia nearly flipped when she found out that her mother had hired Mark Maxwell to dog-sit while the Clinton family went off to a family reunion. Why he was just about the most attractive guy in Blossom Valley High! Now she would have a chance to get to know him.